Carlt

Also by
Carlton Mellick III

THE BIGMEAT

CARLTON MELLICK III

ERASERHEAD PRESS
PORTLAND, OREGON

ERASERHEAD PRESS
205 NE BRYANT
PORTLAND, OR 97211

WWW.ERASERHEADPRESS.COM

ISBN: 978-1-62105-248-7

Copyright © 2017 by Carlton Mellick III

Cover art copyright © 2017 by Ed Mironiuk
www.edmironiuk.com

Printed in the USA.

AUTHOR'S NOTE

I was raised on old Godzilla movies. Back when I was a kid in the 1980's, the best part of the weekend wasn't Saturday morning cartoons. It was the old Godzilla movies they played on Saturday afternoon after the cartoons were over. I have carried a fondness for those cheesy old movies most of my life and love the fact that they still make them to this day. The kaiju genre has kind of exploded in recent years, ever since *Pacific Rim* was released in 2013, and I hope it continues this way for as long as possible. I really don't think I could ever get sick of giant monsters rampaging through cities.

For years, I've been thinking about writing my own giant monster book, but I just had way too many other projects in the works and this one kept getting pushed back year after year. There was a time when a Godzilla-esque giant monster novel was practically unheard of. I kind of wish I would've written this back then. Now they are pretty much everywhere. I think I might be the last small press genre writer to do a giant monster book unless you count *Bio Melt* or *Warrior Wolf Women of the Wasteland* as giant monster books (which I don't, despite the presence of large rampaging creatures). I almost decided never to write one at all.

But then I came up with an idea for a book that really inspired me called *The Cleanup Crew*. It was kind of a parody of a giant monster story. Instead of focusing on the giant monster attack, I wanted it to be about the aftermath of the attack, taking place long after the giant monster was killed. I wanted it to be a story about people living in a destroyed city with a 10,000-ton biohazard of a corpse rotting away for weeks or months and not knowing what the hell to do with it. The concept went through multiple different incarnations over the years. At one point, I even considered making it a typical romantic comedy that just happened to take place in a world with giant monsters. I also thought of making it a serious drama about the working class dealing with giant corpse cleanup duty. In the end, I settled on the book you hold in your hands, now titled *The Big Meat*.

I hope you enjoy reading this book as much as I enjoyed writing it. There's a chance I might write more giant monster books in the future. I only used a few ideas out of the hundreds I came up with during the course of writing this book. For instance, there are no giant robots in The Big Meat. I could do a shitload with giant robots. I'm pretty sure my fucking spirit animal is a giant robot. This needs to happen.

—Carlton Mellick III 3/29/2017 2:37am

PART ONE
CLOCKING IN

CHAPTER
ONE

There is no part of the city where the corpse is not visible. It can be seen from every window, every street corner. A massive mound of rotting putrid flesh that stretches for miles across the city. It doesn't look like a monster anymore. Its limbs have been cut off. Its wings burnt to twigs of ash. Its head removed, taken by men in black coats so that its surprisingly small brain could be studied in some lab on the east coast. Even the spiny reptilian tail is missing. All that's left is the meat. A mountain of ugly black meat rising into the clouds so high that it blocks out the sun, covering our dilapidated homes in shadow.

The sight of it is horrific, but it is nothing compared to the smell. The reek of decay is everywhere. No matter how tightly you close the windows, no matter how much air freshener you spray, no matter how you try to grow used to the stench, it is always there, lingering. It covers your clothes, your furniture. It's on your wife's crusty dehydrated lips when you kiss her at night. It's in the red paste of every can of cold spaghetti you try to eat.

The corpse was once a symbol to be proud of. A symbol of triumph over impossible odds. Now it's a plague. And even though they've been trying to clear it away for the past four months, the majority of the body still remains, forever obscuring our light.

"Have you ever seen it up close?"

The man with the big gray beard stares at me through his gas mask. I can't quite hear him over the roaring engine of the dump truck as we plow through the rubble. He doesn't look at the road as he drives, just staring at me as I cower in the passenger seat.

I yell over the engine, "What?"

"The Big Meat," he raises his voice, pointing at the black mountain closing in on us. "Ever been this close?"

I shake my head. I've been living in the city with The Meat for all this time, but I've never been within a hundred feet of the rotting mountain. "Not since they killed it."

When I look up at the wall of meat ahead of us, I'm rendered breathless. I go dizzy. It feels like it's coming at us, like a tsunami of rotten black flesh. I can only look at it for a moment before my eyes dart back to my hands in my lap.

"What did they tell you about it?" he asks.

I shrug. "They just said I'll be joining the cleanup crew."

"Which crew? Hide, fat, bone, gas?"

I have no idea what he's talking about. "I don't know. They said I'm on Meri's crew."

"Meri?" The large man bursts into laughter, his mask shaking against his pudgy face. "Are you fucking kidding me?"

His laugh sends shivers down my spine. "What's wrong with Meri's crew?"

"She's gut crew. Nobody wants that job. Man, I'm sorry." He shakes his head in fake sympathy, trying to hold back more laughter. "I can't believe they'd do that to you on your first day."

"They said her crew was severely short-handed."

He nods. "Yeah, they're always short-handed. Most people

on gut crew don't last very long."

"What do you mean they don't last long?"

"Well, being on any cleanup crew is dangerous work, but gut crew is the absolute worst. Every month, about ten people are injured, infected, or killed working this job. Nine out of those ten are usually gut crew."

I slink down in my seat, adjusting my gas mask tighter to my face. I was already terrified of this job. It already took all of my courage just to get out of bed and show up for work that day. The dump truck driver is only making it worse. I pray it's not as bad as he says it is.

"Don't be afraid to quit," says the driver. "If by the end of the day you don't think you can handle it just tell them you refuse to continue. Try to get on another crew. If they won't transfer you then just go home and never come back."

I shake my head. "But they aren't giving away rations anymore. And with the quarantine still in effect, it's not like I have anywhere else to go. This job is the only way I can survive."

The driver lets out a sigh, fogging up his mask. "Have you been listening to what I've been saying? You'd have a better chance of survival by looting and scavving than working gut crew. It's suicide."

"But they shoot looters on sight."

He nods. "Yeah, as I said, you'd have a better chance of survival doing that than on gut crew."

Up ahead, dozens of trucks and excavators have gathered along the massive wall of meat like orange metal ants picking at a deer carcass one tiny piece at a time. The excavators dig into the black rancid flesh, scooping out about 600 pounds of meat at a time, then dropping the hefty chunks into the beds of dump trucks.

"That's my job," the driver says, pointing at the dump

trucks ahead of us. "Waste Disposal. We work mostly with hide crew and fat crew. If you know how to operate heavy machinery, it's one of the easiest and safest jobs here. All I have to do is drive back and forth between The Meat and the incineration pits. It's not bad at all, once you get the hang of it."

I nod at him, perhaps a bit jealous of his job, wondering if I could ever be capable of driving a truck like this. Though they'd probably never put me in such a position. I don't even have a driver's license anymore.

We pass a few dump trucks headed in the opposite direction. The backs of their vehicles filled way past the brim with dozens of chunks of meat. The boulders of fat seem to pulse and squirm against each other, wriggling like they're still alive. It's just the rumbling of the trucks on the dirt road that causes the flesh to move like this, but I still can't help but see them as living.

It's a common fear that people have in this city—the belief that the creature isn't fully dead, that it could come back to life at any minute and continue its rampage. Even after its head and legs were removed, people still can't help but feel this way. The thing seemed unkillable. The military fought it for almost a year as the creature went from city to city, eating and destroying everything in its path. They launched everything they could at it. Missiles, bombs, nuclear warheads. Nothing worked. The thing's hide was tough enough to take anything we could throw at it. A few times, the military was able to bring it down. The thing went limp and collapsed, presumed dead. But it didn't stay dead for long. It had the ability to regenerate itself. No matter how bad the damage, it would always get back up after a couple days of recovery, and then continue on its path of destruction.

When it fell here in Portland, we all thought it would be no different than the time it was taken down in Chicago or outside of Kansas City. We all expected it to eventually get back up and finish the rest of us off. But it's been over four months and there's no sign of regeneration. They say the thing is completely dead now and there's no chance of it coming back. But fear isn't rational. It doesn't answer to logic. And a lot of people still believe it could come back to life any day now, especially those who survived close encounters with the creature. People like me.

I remember when the monster first appeared in the mountains of Colorado. The news reports didn't seem real. Nobody believed it. We watched with big smiles on our faces, like all the news organizations were in on a joke, trying to create another *War of the Worlds* as Orson Welles did on Halloween night in 1938. For the first few days, it was just entertainment. Everyone watched it like a scripted reality television show. Even when they insisted it was all real, we still thought it had to be a joke. The monster even looked like it came straight from an old Japanese Kaiju film, like the perfect mixture between Godzilla and King Ghidorah, only ten times bigger.

My mother wouldn't even come into the living room when they first started reporting on it, assuming the media had sunk to an all-time low. Bill Cosby, Miley Cyrus, and Donald Trump were bad enough. Now they had to focus on this bullshit? She wanted to throw the television out the window and be done with it.

"But it's on all the channels," David said, snickering with glee. "CNN says it came from some deep cave system beneath the Earth's mantle. Fox News is trying to blame Obama."

Ever since he dropped out of college and moved back home, my older brother was always sitting in front of the television, drinking cheap beer and growing out his hipster beard. He didn't have a job or any plans to get one soon. He didn't even clean up after himself anymore.

"It's shooting blue fire from its mouth," he shook his head and took another swig of Hamm's.

I sat next to him, only partially watching the news in the background while trying to study for the SATs. My parents were putting extra pressure on me, determined to make sure I didn't end up like my brother. What they didn't realize was that their pressure was most likely what made David the way he was. If he was never going to meet their high expectations then why bother trying? But they had nothing to worry about with me. I was a decent student and planned to take college seriously, majoring in something I was comfortable with like graphic design or computer art. Even if I dropped out, there was no way I would move back home. I planned to go to school out of state after graduating so I wouldn't have to deal with their judgment ever again. I couldn't wait to get out of that place.

"That thing is kind of awesome," David said, pointing at the television, trying to get my attention off of my studies so that I could watch the monster with him. "I wish it was real."

For the next seventy hours, we watched the news off and on with half-interest, just waiting around for the moment when they announced it was all a joke. But that moment never came. We finally believed it to be real when my cousin Corey called, saying that his father was killed by the thing while on a company trip in Aspen. My dad was torn up by his brother's death, but he didn't have time to grieve. There was no funeral planned. We were all too concerned with the reality of the situation. If that thing actually existed what were we going to do? What if there were more of them?

Would it mean the end of the human race?

We watched the news with bated breaths as it wiped out every major city along I-25. Colorado Springs, Denver, Boulder, Fort Collins. The cities tried to evacuate people, but they only clogged the highway all across the state, creating a trail of bread crumbs for the monster to follow from city to city.

We wondered what would happen if the thing came to Oregon. Could the military actually stop it? Would we be able to flee north to Washington or Canada in time? We considered moving across the globe, to Australia or Thailand. But my parents didn't want to quit their jobs. They didn't want to give up their lives just in the off chance that the creature came to our town.

Luckily, the monster headed east after decimating Colorado, avoiding the Pacific Northwest for the time being. We thought we'd be safe. We thought they'd kill the thing long before it made it back to our side of the country. But after a month of destruction, we learned that there was no place that was safe from the giant creature. It could fly faster than any plane and landed in cities almost at random. You never knew exactly where it would strike next.

I dropped out of school a week before finals. Pretty much everyone did. My parents didn't object. I didn't even bother telling them and they never bothered to ask. My dad didn't officially quit his job, but he stopped going to the office. There just wasn't much for him to do as a stockbroker while the country was collapsing around us. My mom, my dad and I all found ourselves spending our time sitting on the couch next to my brother, drinking beer and growing out our beards. Just waiting until our city was the next to be attacked.

As the dump truck pulls up to the mountain of meat, I panic. My breath becomes rapid. Everything inside of me is screaming, begging me to get out of the truck and run.

The driver sees me squirming as he turns off the engine. He puts his hand on my shoulder and says, "Don't worry, kid. Everyone's terrified on their first day."

We get out and walk to the back of the truck. I don't look at The Meat behind me, trying to keep my eyes off of it. Even through the gas mask, I can smell the rot. I hold the mask tight to my face, worried that the toxic fumes are leaking in, worried about all of the diseases I could get by ingesting too much of the gas.

"Meri's crew should be about ten minutes down the road," the driver says, pointing south. "Just look for a woman with gray dreadlocks. You'll find her."

I look down the road. There's no sign of people in the direction he pointed. Just a bunch of construction equipment.

"But…" I begin.

Before I can ask my question, he says, "Good luck." Then he walks away, heading toward a small crowd of workers gathered at a nearby crane.

Lost and alone. This is how I always feel on the first day of any job I've ever had. But it's even worse this time. I'm less than ten yards from the creature that wiped out two-thirds of the population, including my parents, my friends, and pretty much every single person I ever knew.

My hands shake so much that I have to put them in my pockets. My breath is so rapid inside my mask that my goggles become foggy. I take a few steps in the direction the driver pointed out, but then pause and look back. The other workers ignore me. They walk back and forth between machines—most of them specifically designed for digging and drilling at the endless mass of flesh.

I feel like running. The Meat is so close. I can almost feel warmth issuing from it, even though it's as cold and dead as any corpse. With all of my courage, I turn my eyes to The Meat and get a good look at it. The flesh is hard and rubbery, dried in the sun like beef jerky. High in the air, at the top of The Meat, I can see the black scales of its outer skin. There are people up there, members of the hide crew, cutting through the thick scales with drill-like machines. Helicopters hover overhead, airlifting the pieces of hide one chunk at a time.

The driver said gut crew is the worst, but I couldn't imagine what could be worse than hide crew. They spend their day working on top of The Meat, right at the edge of the cliff. The wall of flesh is as high as two skyscrapers stacked on top of each other. I couldn't imagine having to work at such a height. It has to be a dangerous job. Yet gut crew is supposed to be even worse? I really don't know if I'll be able to manage this job.

Two dump trucks roar to my position, forcing me to move. I sprint out of their way, moving in the direction the driver told me to go. I still don't see anyone up ahead, but I keep walking, hoping I'll find Meri's crew eventually.

The ground beneath my feet is black and coated in a hard slime. This area used to be covered in meat at one time, before it had been cleaned away. It's crazy to think of how much of the corpse has already been removed yet how much of it still exists. It seems like it will take years to eradicate the rest of the corpse. The job is about as difficult as it would be to level all of Mount St. Helens to the ground—if the mountain happened to be covered in a hide as strong as fifty-inch steel.

I walk for twenty minutes and still don't find any sign of

other people. It's just me walking along the black slime road between the massive wall of meat and the miles of rubble that were once the downtown industrial area. I decide that I don't care if I ever find my crew. I'll just walk along The Meat all day until I eventually reach the other side of town, then I'll walk back and go home. If they fire me I'll be happy.

Patting a pack of cigarettes inside of my pants pocket, I wonder if it's possible to smoke while wearing a gas mask. It's the first time I've been able to calm down since I woke up this morning. A cigarette would help even more. I wasn't a smoker until a few weeks ago. Staying in a house that isn't mine—the owners either died or abandoned it a long time ago—I found a carton of cigarettes hidden in the attic. At the time, it was like finding gold. Cigarettes are rare and I knew I could trade them for quite a bit of food and water if I found the right person. But instead of looking for a buyer, worried that they'd just get stolen if I asked the wrong person, I decided to try smoking for the first time in my life. My mother was really strict when it came to smoking. As an ex-smoker, she absolutely despised the habit. Drinking, smoking pot, even taking mushrooms—my mother forgave all of these when my brother was caught with them when he was a teenager. But she freaked out when she caught him smoking. Smoking kills is what she always said. Yeah, maybe smoking is horrible for your health and will eventually kill you, but after all I'd been through I realized that life is too short. Getting any enjoyment out of life, no matter how small or how big the consequence, was worth it. So many health-conscious non-smokers died in the monster attacks. Avoiding tobacco did not save them. They could have smoked every day of their lives and the result would've been the same. That's why I decided to light that first cigarette. And while it took a couple dozen before I grew to enjoy them—just using them as a means to suppress hunger—smoking has become my favorite part of the day. Something to look forward to. Something to save and relish. It's funny how something that will surely kill me has given me a reason to live.

I decide not to light up. I would be so worried about lifting my gas mask, even in brief moments, that I wouldn't be able to enjoy it. If I tried to smoke through the mask's filter it would probably just be a waste of both the cigarette and the filter. Also, I've been told that the gasses The Meat emits are highly flammable. And with all the gas collected in the monster's guts, one spark and the whole thing could explode. At least that's what people have said. They didn't warn me about open flames before I arrived, so maybe it's not as big of an issue as I've heard. Still, I would kill for a cigarette about now.

A small group of people appears ahead of me. I'm not sure if they're my crew. If they are, they're much farther down than the driver told me they'd be. They wear airtight yellow rubber suits, different than the gray jumpsuit I'm wearing. They huddle around a makeshift shed and a few large drill-shaped machines that are like cone-shaped tractors with tank tread wheels. Only one of the three seems to be functional. The other two appear broken down and stripped for parts.

The workers don't acknowledge me as I approach. One of them, a man with a long white beard dangling below his mask, glances at me briefly, but doesn't say anything or point me out to the others. I examine all the workers as I come closer. None of them look female, let alone have gray dreadlocks. They're all much larger and older than I am. The youngest is probably in his late thirties, early forties. The weakest could still probably bench twice my weight. Even the old guy with the white beard could break me in half with his little finger. I wonder if they're the right group.

"Is this Meri's crew?" I ask them as I arrive.

They don't even look at me, busy pulling tools and equipment from the shed. I wonder if my voice was muffled by my mask.

I speak louder, "I'm looking for Meri."

That time I could tell they heard me and just purposely ignored me. It's like they each hope somebody else will deal with me, like talking to me isn't a part of their job description and they don't deal with a single thing outside of that job description.

"I've been assigned to Meri's crew," I say.

That gets their attention. They all stop what they're doing and look at me. Their eyes beam on me with anger and disgust. I'm taken aback, wondering what I've done wrong.

My voice stutters. "Is she here?"

They still don't speak. The closest worker, a man with dark skin and sunken eyes, points at the shed. I look at the metal structure, then back at him with a questioning face. But he doesn't nod in confirmation.

The workers watch me as I step cautiously to the shed. It seems like I've got the right crew, but the idea of working with this angry group is even more frightening than The Big Meat itself. My very presence seems to irritate them to no end. I've never felt like I belonged somewhere less than I do right here, right now.

Inside the shed, all I see are shelves of supplies and a pile of random buckets and tools in the center of the floor. I look back at the workers but they've already lost interest in me, talking to each other in angry tones. One of them turns away and kicks a black rock across the ground. I can't help but think it's my presence that has upset them. Or maybe they're just always in that bad of a mood.

I step inside the shed and find a woman around the corner, sitting at a small desk, filling out paperwork. That area of the shed is like a small office with three filing cabinets and a bulletin board. Sticky notes posted everywhere. A laptop lies beneath a mountain of folders, looking like it hasn't been used in months. The small generator next to her also looks like it hasn't been used in a long time, probably doesn't even work anymore. The lights in the room are dark. I have no idea how she can even see.

"You're blocking the light," she says, a coarse smoker's voice.

I step away from the door, deeper into the shed so that the small amount of sunlight can shine in on her. She doesn't turn around to greet me. Just sitting there and continuing her work, too focused to say anything. I just wait, not wanting to interrupt her, not sure what else to do. I only see her from behind. She wears battered tan overalls on top of a grubby white tank top. Her arms are bare and filthy. Her hair—black and gray dreadlocks that stretch down her back—are even worse. She probably hasn't bathed in a very long time. Not because baths are hard to come by, but because she just doesn't give a shit.

After ten minutes of standing here like an idiot, I decide I probably should say something. She obviously hears me standing behind her, shuffling back and forth, clearing my throat, playing with the jellybeans in my pockets—the only thing I had to bring for lunch.

"Umm…" I begin, but then fall quiet as she lets out a long irritated sigh.

"If you need something, speak up," she says. "I'm behind schedule."

"You're Meri?" I ask, even though I know the answer.

"No, I'm Cactus Jack."

I pause in confusion. I'm not sure if that's supposed to be some kind of joke. Isn't Cactus Jack an old professional wrestler? Why would she say that?

I say, "They told me to find Meri."

She still doesn't look up from her paperwork. "What do they want this time? If it's extra drill bits, tell them they can go fuck themselves. I don't have any to spare."

"No," I say. "They said I'm assigned to your crew."

The pen freezes in her hand, then she slams it on the desk. "Are you fucking with me?"

She turns around and glares in my direction. One look with her piercing brown eyes and I step back and nearly knock down all the contents of the shelves behind me. There's something fierce about the woman. Something that makes me cower at the sight of her. The angry old guys outside are mere puppy dogs compared to her. She's half the size of the smallest guy out there, but she looks tough enough to kick all of their asses at once. I can't make out her age. She's got deep wrinkles in her face, like a woman in her late forties, yet her body and posture are more like that of a girl in her twenties. I'm not sure if she's an older woman who's aged really well or a young woman who's aged quickly. My bet is on the latter. The last year and a half has been rough enough to age anyone ten years at the least.

"You better be fucking with me…" she says.

"Yeah, I…" I choke on my words. "That's what they told me."

She throws her head back, her dreads whipping in one large matted chunk. "I can't fucking believe it. How old are you, anyway? Do you even have pubes yet?"

"I'm eighteen," I say. I don't bother mentioning that I've only been eighteen for a few weeks. "I look kind of young for my age."

She sneers. "Kind of? You'd look young for a twelve-year-old."

I'm not sure why she has to be so insulting. It's not like I had any choice in the matter. I just went where they told me to go.

"I told them to send me five *experienced* guys," she continues. "And what do I get? A kid barely out of diapers?"

I don't know what to say. I just break eye contact, look at the floor. I've never been good at this kind of confrontation.

"What crew did they transfer you from?" she asks.

"It's my first day."

She shakes her head. "Of course it is. Did they give you any training?"

I shrug.

"Of course they didn't," she says.

I say, "I read a printout they gave me at the interview," but she doesn't bother listening to me.

"Have you even worked a job a day in your life?"

I think about it for a minute, wondering if I should make something up. All my friends worked through high school, usually at ice cream shops or in the food court at the mall. But my parents never wanted me to work. They wanted me to focus on school. They also liked controlling me with an allowance. If I wanted to buy something, they'd get to decide whether or not I should have it. If I wanted to borrow the car, they got to decide where I went or how long I was gone. Getting a job would mean freedom from their control and that's something they didn't want to give up. But I actually did try to work at several different jobs in the past, usually during the summer when I didn't have school work. I wouldn't call those real jobs, though. I always quit soon after training.

I say, "I've had lots of jobs. McDonald's, Taco Bell, the car wash, the gas station, telemarketing. I even used to wash dishes at my grandma's restaurant when I was a kid."

I don't mention that the longest I lasted at any of those jobs was two weeks, and that was the one at my grandma's restaurant when I was ten years old. But even with the long list of summer jobs, Meri wasn't impressed. I might as well have told her I never worked a day in my life.

She smiles at me in the dismissive way a 3rd grade teacher might do to a student that's annoying her. "Wait one minute. I'll get this sorted."

Then she picks up her walkie-talkie, asking for a guy named Frank. I believe he's the guy who hired me, though I never spoke to him directly. I was interviewed by his secretary.

The first thing she says when he picks up is, "Have you made funeral arrangements yet? Because I *am* going to murder you. This time for real."

They argue back and forth over the walkie for what seems like half an hour. Meri just yells at him, telling him about how I'm going to get myself killed or get her team killed and how she's going to kill him if he doesn't give her some real workers. But the guy on the other line doesn't budge. He says he can't afford to transfer anyone and all the new hires are just as inexperienced as I am. Until the quarantine goes down and they're able to bring in workers from other cities, which is something that won't happen anytime soon if it ever happens at all, they're stuck with whoever they can get.

When the conversation is over, she drops the walkie-talkie on her desk and goes back to her paperwork. I don't know if she resolved anything or not. She just ignores me like a problem she hopes will just go away, like she's hoping I'll walk off the job and never return. It's something I'm strongly considering doing, but for some reason I can't muster the courage to leave.

When she finally speaks to me again, Meri says, "Suit up. We go in two minutes."

She doesn't tell me what she means by *suit up*. I assume she wants me to put on one of the yellow jumpsuits the other workers are wearing. I see one hanging from a coat rack.

I go to it, pick it up off the hook, trying to figure out how to get inside of the thing. There's no sign of a zipper or any noticeable way to open it. I'm not even sure if I should take off my clothes or wear them underneath. She doesn't volunteer this information.

Struggling to get into the rubber suit, sticking my leg down the neck hole, completely aware of how idiotic I must look.

When I nearly fall over, unable to balance on one leg, knocking into the nearby shelves, Meri turns around and groans out loud.

"Not that one," she yells.

She gets up from her desk and stomps toward me, pulling the suit from my hands. She looks at it, wiping away the crap I rubbed onto it with my shoes. I feel like an even bigger idiot than ever when I realize that the suit I was trying to put on is hers.

"It's in here," she says. She goes to the supplies, opens a box from the bottom shelf, and pulls out a new rubber suit, folded and packaged in shrink wrap. "This is the smallest size we got."

When she hands it to me, I wonder how the heck she expected me to find it on my own. All she said was *suit up* and expected me to know what to do from there? Did she do that on purpose to make me feel stupid? To test me? I hate how supervisors always treat you like you're an idiot for not knowing things you couldn't possibly know yet. It's happened at every job I've ever had. It's why I always quit within two weeks of being hired.

When Meri puts on her jumpsuit, I watch carefully, learning how to open the thing, unzipping it from the inside front. We don't have to take anything off, not even our shoes, even though the suit has built in galoshes.

Once I've pulled it on, Meri zips me up like a mother dressing her child for the first day of kindergarten.

She pulls the hood over my head and says, "Don't let any of that stuff get inside."

"What stuff?" I ask.

She doesn't answer, just saying, "It's toxic. Even if you don't have any open wounds, it'll cause infection if it gets on your skin. If you have to get a limb amputated you'll be useless to us." Then she adds, "*More* useless."

"What stuff?" I repeat.

She says, "All of it. All the stuff."

But I still don't understand what she means.

As I exit the shed, my new suit makes a squeaking noise with every step I take. I'm the only one who squeaks, though. Meri's suit is so worn in that it only makes a whooshing sound.

Meri doesn't stay by my side, pushing forward to her crew, moving on with her duties. She didn't even bother getting my name.

"Let's move out," she says.

But the others don't want to go. They still seem peeved over my presence among them.

"Is this maggot really going in there with us?" asks one of the workers. A black man with a thick accent. I can't tell his ethnicity for sure, but if I had to guess I'd say he was American Samoan.

"Yep," Meri responds, practically dismissing the Samoan as she heads for the large drill-like machine.

"He's going to get us killed," he says.

"Yeah, this is some bullshit, Meri," says the old guy with the white beard. His voice has the guttural twang of an Alabama coal miner.

"Deal with it," she says.

It's all she has to say to shut them up. They know better than to push the matter with her.

Meri climbs up into the seat of the drill-tractor-thing and turns on the engine. She looks back at the Samoan, who is still grumbling to himself and kicking slime rocks.

Meri tells him, "You're on the grinder."

By the look on his face, I can tell that she just gave him a job that nobody wants. It's his reward for sulking. The Samoan doesn't object, but it's obvious that he's twice as pissed as before.

Instead of arguing with the crew leader, the Samoan turns

his frustration on me. He shoves his equipment in my face.

"Carry our shit, Maggot," he says to me, piling as much stuff as possible into my arms.

I just stay silent and let him give me whatever stuff he wants to give me. Shovels, tools, vinyl bags filled with what feels like fifty-pound lead weights. It's three times more than I can realistically carry, but I don't protest. The other workers follow suit and hand me even more stuff to carry.

It's supposed to be their payback. Since they're stuck with me, they think I at least owe it to them to lighten their load. But once I drop their stuff in the slimy dirt, they realize the mistake they made and take half of their equipment back.

The Samoan goes to a machine along the side of the shed, a smaller vehicle I hadn't seen before. I instantly understand why they call it the grinder. The machine looks like a meat grinder on wheels.

Meri drives the drilling machine forward, heading south along the wall of meat. The Samoan follows in the grinder. Both machines move slowly, tractor-speed. The rest of us are supposed to follow on foot.

"Let's go, Maggot," says a man from behind, his voice almost cheerful.

I turn around to see the largest, scariest-looking worker among them. A Hispanic man with cheeks so large they squish into the sides of his gasmask. He glares at me. The big smile on his face offsets his intimidating appearance. I wonder if he's friendlier than the others.

"Why do you guys keep calling me maggot?" I ask him.

When his smile leaves his face, I realize he's not quite as friendly as I hoped.

"Because that's what you are," he says. "All the new guys are called maggots until they prove themselves."

I guess it makes sense. But I don't understand why all the

workers don't think of themselves as maggots as well. We're all like maggots compared to the giant rotting corpse.

"So what do you call me if I prove myself?" I ask. "Do I become a fly?"

The large man laughs and shakes his head. "You'll die long before you prove yourself. The last maggot didn't last a week and he had ten years construction experience. You're going to beat his record for sure."

I shake my head, wondering what the hell I'm doing here. The dump truck driver was right. I'm probably better off looting than doing this job. But I don't have the courage to just walk away. If I'm going to quit it will have to be tomorrow, when I don't bother showing up.

Up ahead, Meri turns the driller into the meat. At first, I thought she was going to drill into the side of the flesh wall, but she doesn't turn on the drill. There's already a hole. It's like a mineshaft in the meat. She drives into it. The Samoan follows in the grinder.

My heart squeezes in my chest.

"Wait," I say. "We're going in *there?*"

The Hispanic man giggles. "Of course. Where did you think we worked? Our job is to clean out the intestines and internal organs."

"I hope you're not claustrophobic," the old guy says, appearing on my right, listening in on our conversation.

"Fuck that," I say.

The workers around me laugh, getting pleasure from watching me squirm. It's good to know that my misery is the only thing that brightens their sour mood.

When we step up to the entrance to the mineshaft, I peer down the tunnel of rotten flesh. It goes far deeper than my eyes can see, miles into the meat mountain. It's like I'm staring down the throat of the giant beast.

Then the stench hits. Even through the gas mask, it overwhelms me. I bite my tongue to prevent myself from vomiting and try breathing only through my mouth. It doesn't help. I've smelled dead rabbits, dead snakes, dead fish, even a dead cow once. But no smell of death compares to this. I can't believe I have to actually step inside of it, spend a whole day bathing in the foul stink.

When he sees the look of fear and disgust in my eyes as I stand frozen at the maw-like entrance to the cave, the large Hispanic man slaps me on the back so hard I nearly drop all the shovels in my arms.

"Welcome to gut crew," he says.

CHAPTER
TWO

The creature didn't have an official name. All the media outlets tossed a new name out there on a weekly basis, trying to get something to stick. But they couldn't come up with anything appropriate, anything that would catch on. *Rexzilla* was the first name they used. It was meant to be a combination of Tyrannosaurus Rex and Godzilla. But the monster was far larger than both of those creatures, and it was neither extinct nor fictional. Then they used *Gargantus*, then *Colossus*, then *Gargotheron*, *Mammothra*, then *King Titan*, then *The City Smasher*, and the last one I remember was *Armageddon Dragon*. But in the end, they realized all the names they came up with were just too cartoonish, too tacky, too insulting to the families of all those people who died. There was no name that could describe such a massive force. No name that would do it justice. By the time the thing wiped out New York City, the media stopped trying to give it a name. From that point on, the thing was just referred to as *the monster, the creature, the beast*, or just plain *it*.

But some people had their own private nicknames for the creature. The military's nickname for it was *Manny*, so some people called it that. I have no idea why they called it Manny. Short for *Maneater* maybe? Not sure. My friends from school referred to it as *The Lizard*, though we didn't know if it was actually reptilian. My brother came up with the name *Grim*, because he had an ugly black metal friend who went by that name and bore a slight resemblance to the thing, at least in the facial area. So that's what my family called the creature.

At first it was just a joke, but over time we realized that Grim was the only possible name for the creature. The thing really was like a Grim Reaper, harvesting human lives all across the countryside. The name was so apt that it wasn't just contained to my family. Our neighbors, my brother's friends, my parent's coworkers— everyone who heard the monster referred to as The Reaper immediately adapted to the nickname. It was the only title that made sense. Because by that time, after so many major cities collapsed beneath the heels of the beast, everyone was thinking the same thing: *Death is coming*. Not a monster. Not a force of nature. But Death itself.

Walking through the tunnel of rotting flesh, I can't believe I'm actually inside it. Inside *The Reaper*. The monster that came so close to ravishing the entire world. The thought is too much for me to bear, so I attempt to block it from my mind. I try to think of it as just an ordinary cave, like I'm just a lowly coal miner off to mine for coal. The charade lasts for only about two minutes.

"How deep does it go?" I ask the others, trying to suppress nausea.

The old guy is the closest to me, so I look at him, waiting for an answer. He tries to ignore me, but I just ask again. I would have asked the slightly friendlier Hispanic man, but he's two people behind me, picking up the rear.

The old guy eventually gives in. He groans and says, "We're going about eight or nine miles in."

My eyes bulge. "That far? Are you serious?"

As the darkness floods in, I see the other workers turning lights on their rubber suits. They don't use headlights as miners would use on their helmets. Instead, their suits are equipped with string lights along the seams that illuminate their entire suit. Iridescent green light issues from them like their whole bodies are covered in glow sticks. I try to search for the on switch on my suit, but I can't figure it out.

"How do you work the light?" I ask the old guy.

He groans at me again. Then he grabs the collar of my suit and flips a switch. My body glows green. It takes a few minutes for it to fully brighten. Maybe because it's a new suit.

"Thanks," I say to him. "By the way, what's your name?"

The old guy has obviously had enough of answering my questions. "Fuck off. That's my name."

"Sorry…" I say, wondering how I offended him.

He grumbles to himself for a bit and then quickens his pace, trying to create distance between us.

The large Hispanic man two people back was listening in on our conversation. He shouts up to me, "Don't take it personally, kid. We make it a point not to get too attached to maggots around here. It makes it easier for us once you get yourself killed."

Twenty minutes of walking and I can no longer see the exit of the cave. The tunnel seems to tighten, close in on me. At first I think it's my imagination, but then I realize the walls are mere inches away from the sides of the grinder ahead of me, where there originally were a few feet of wiggle room. My breath becomes thick in my mask. My muscles tighten. I've always been uncomfortable in tight spaces. If the tunnel stayed the same width as it was when we entered, then I wouldn't have a problem. But a narrowing tunnel freaks me out. It makes me imagine how tight it might get up ahead. Will it squeeze all the way to my shoulders? Will I have to walk sideways? The fact that I can't run away is what is most unnerving to me. There are people behind me, pushing me forward. I'm carrying their supplies, so I can't just drop it all and run away. I have to at least get to the end of the tunnel.

The deeper in we go, the fouler the stench becomes. I'm the only one suffering from it, though. I gag and choke and dry heave in my mask, but the others are perfectly composed, as though they are completely used to it now. I never thought it possible to get used to the stench, even when experiencing it from miles away. These guys must be resilient as fuck to be capable of dealing with this on a daily basis. Even though they're all a bunch of grumpy assholes, I'm envious of their resolve.

The ground grows softer as we walk. Squishing beneath our boots with every step, like walking through wet mud after a hard rain. Once my feet begin sinking into the rotten goo, up to my ankles in parts, I understand why we're wearing these rubber suits. This stuff gets everywhere. All of it toxic and bacteria ridden. One spoonful of that stuff could kill me if it gets into my suit, yet here I am practically wading through it. This is surely going to be one of the most miserable days of my life.

The walls pulse and writhe around me inside the monster's corpse. It's like the thing is breathing. I felt the same way outside, like the creature is regenerating, trying to come back to life. But that's not it. There's something inside the meat that makes it move.

"Watch the worms," somebody calls out, far ahead of me.

The old guy repeats, looking down at his feet. "Worms."

I don't know what he's talking about until I see them. The guy behind me grabs me by the shoulder, stopping me just in time. At my feet, there are three large parasites. Worm-like creatures the size of boa constrictors with large hook-like teeth.

"What the fuck are those?" I cry, inching backward.

"Tack worms," says the Hispanic guy. "Stay away from them."

The guy holding my shoulder says, "They'll chew right through your suit."

The things coil in the wet gore, making a barking hissing sound similar to that of a badger. Looking closer, they're more like eels or giant lampreys than worms.

"The deeper in you go, the more you'll find," says the man behind me. "They're one of the many things that can kill you inside The Meat."

I step around the tack worms, keeping clear of their hissing piranha mouths.

"What else can kill you in here?" I ask.

"Pretty much everything," the large Hispanic man says. "The bugs, the gas, the acid, the equipment."

"Meri," one of them adds.

"Yeah," the Hispanic man says. "Meri will kill you if you piss her off enough."

I can't tell if he's joking about that or not. The words sound like he's joking around, but the serious tone of his voice, and the way everyone else goes silent after he says it, sounds like there could be a bit of truth in what he's saying. Perhaps she has killed workers in the past. Or at least has been responsible for some of their deaths in some way or another. Ordering somebody to do a job that gets them killed is close to murdering them.

We arrive in a large cavity in the creature's abdomen. It's about the size of a large movie theater or high school gym. The walls here are different than the tunnel. They're not muscle. They're intestine. Massive coiling tubes like white water slides cover the walls around of us.

"Welcome to the pit," the large Hispanic man says, rubbing the squeaky rubber hood on my head.

The pit. It's a perfect name for this cavity. We descend a slope, twenty feet down to the soggy bottom of the chamber. I slip twice trying to get down, nearly dropping all the gear in my arms. But I catch myself each time. There's no way I'm falling into that liquid rot on the floor.

The most surprising thing to find inside the meat cave is a small building. Somebody put together a little metal room, maybe an office or a break room. Meri pulls the driller up to the side of the room and gets off. The Samoan parks the grinder next to her. When she gets to the side of the building, she flips a switch, brightening the cavity with flood lights.

"Bring that shit inside," the old guy tells me once I get to the bottom of the slope, pointing at the room.

I nod and go in. The room has its own generator and fluorescent lighting. Three tables and chairs. A couple shelves of extra supplies. A bulletin board. It does look a bit like a break room, but I think it's more than that. It seems like a safe room. There are oxygen tanks and canned food and water. If the doors are sealed it can probably be a safe place to remove your gas mask. Though probably not your whole suit. The floor is covered in slime tracked in on people's boots. It's probably only used in an emergency.

When I get inside, I drop everything on the ground and wheeze with relief. The other three guys in the room with me turn their eyes at the clanging sound of shovels hitting the metal floor, glaring at me like I just committed a great offense against them by dropping their gear, but I don't care. I stretch out my arms and catch my breath. I feel like just carrying this stuff and walking eight miles through the corpse was enough to wipe me out for the day. I'm ready to go home and take a nap, but we haven't even started work yet.

"Hey Maggot," says the large Hispanic man on the other side of the room. "Come here."

I look at him. He's standing by the bulletin board with a Polaroid camera in his hands.

When I go to him, he says, "Stand there." Then he takes my picture.

As he shakes the developing image in his hand, he says, "It's for the wall."

I look at the bulletin board to see a large collection of photographs. All the workers on gut crew. They are separated into two sections: the living and the dead. The Hispanic guy posts my picture in the living section. It is much smaller than the section of the dead. Only seven images, compared to the fifty or more who have died on the job.

"Write your name on it if you want," he says, handing me a pen.

Then he turns on a small battery-operated candle on the shelf below the images, makes a cross on his chest, and walks away.

I look at all the photographs. So many people died on this job. Mostly men, but there are a few women among the dead. All of them older and more fit than I am. No young teenaged slackers in the bunch.

As I write my name below my picture, I examine the names of my seven co-workers, trying to attach names to faces and commit them to memory. I immediately recognize a few of them. Meri, the only woman, is the easiest to spot. Then the large Hispanic guy, whose name is Sanchez. The old guy with the white beard is named Bill. The Samoan guy's name is Hoji. There's a guy named Hector. I think he was the guy walking behind me in the tunnel, the guy with the dark complexion and sunken eyes. The other two guys I don't recognize at all. A large bald white guy named Mitch and a large bald black guy named Jake. I'm not sure they're even on the job today. There were about seven other workers that came down here with me, I'm pretty sure, so they're probably here somewhere. It couldn't be their day off. They told me that we don't get days off unless we're injured.

"Where's the maggot?" I hear Meri shouting deep outside the room. Her voice is angry, as though I've already done something wrong.

I rush out the door and head toward her. But she doesn't speak. She just stares at me, waiting for me to get close. She doesn't say whatever it is she has to say to me. It makes me wonder if I imagined her calling for me at all. I stand facing her. She glares at me. No words are exchanged. Maybe she just wants to keep track of me.

She breaks eye contact and leans her walkie-talkie into her hip. Then she turns her attention to another worker as he approaches. The one called Hector.

"Disposal said they'll be another ten minutes," he says, approaching us with hoses and tubes draped over his shoulders.

Meri nods. "Well, let's get started."

She turns to the rest of the crew and raises her voice so

they could all hear her from anywhere within the cavity.

"Today's quota is thirty feet off the southwest quadrant," she says.

"Thirty feet?" the old guy, Bill, complains. His voice too quiet for Meri to hear. "With only one grinder?"

"Jake, you're on the drill. Hector, suction. Mitch, excavation. The rest of you are tossing shit."

The crew breaks up and prepares to get to work.

Meri takes a coil of rubber tubing from Hector and says, "Maggot, come with me."

I follow her to an open space away from the machines. She tosses the tubing on the ground and says, "Cut this into eight-inch strips and put them in that bucket." She nods toward a gore-caked paint bucket, then walks away.

I look down at the tubing, then at the bucket, then back at her. But she's already gone on to other duties. The tube is clean and new, coiled in a circle like a brand new garden hose. It would probably be about thirty feet long if it was stretched out. Does she really want me to cut it up? What possible purpose would they need this cut for? If I cut it up and then find out that I misheard her—like maybe she asked me to fold it up or something—isn't she going to be pissed at me for ruining it? I just look down at the loops of rubber, not sure what to do. I don't even have anything to cut it with.

"What do I do?" I ask the guy next to me. I'm not sure who it is. His back is turned so all I see is the yellow suit.

He doesn't turn around.

I go into the safe room, looking for something to cut the tubes with. Hoji is in there, going through the equipment I carried through the tunnel. If there's anything I can use to cut the tube with it would likely be in one of these bags. Unfortunately, most of it is Hoji's equipment and he's the last guy I want to bother for help. He's got to be the biggest asshole in the group.

I go toward him, but keep my distance. As he digs through the bags on the table, removing strange tools and machine parts that don't serve any purpose I can comprehend, I try to spot knives, sheers, or anything that I can use to cut rubber tubes.

"What the fuck do you want?" he asks.

I planned to just stay quiet and wait for him to finish, but since he asked I don't have a choice but to speak up.

"Got a utility knife in there?" I ask.

"Yeah, I got a knife for you," he says in a threatening tone.

I go to him, wondering if he's actually going to be helpful. The second I rest my hands on the table, he stabs the blade of the knife into the wood, missing my small finger by less than an inch. I jump back in surprise. Even if the thing didn't stab me, it could have cut a hole in my glove. I'm not entirely sure if he missed on purpose.

But if he's giving me the knife, I can't get angry with him. I need it to do my job.

I go to grab the utility knife out of the table, but he takes it back before I can wrap my fingers around it.

"I said I had a knife," he says. "I didn't say you could use it."

He folds up the blade and puts it into a slot on his belt. Then he walks away, carrying most of the equipment with him. Now that I think about it, all of the workers were wearing tool belts. They probably all have knives on them. But I didn't get a belt. I don't have the same tools. I wonder if Meri expected me to grab one back in the shed outside of The Meat, but failed to tell me to do so. That could have been why she expected me to separate the tubing without giving me anything to cut it with.

Digging through the only bag Hoji left behind, I don't come across an extra knife like the one the workers carry in their tool belt. But there is a box cutter. It's old and rusted and probably wouldn't cleanly cut through even paper, but at least it's something.

When I exit the safe room, I realize that Hector is already cutting up the tubing for me. He's slicing it up with his utility knife so fast that he's able to get three pieces per cut, which then drop down into the bucket at his feet. I go to him, just watching him do the job.

"What are you cutting that for?" I ask him.

He just says, "Put them in the bucket," but doesn't exactly answer my question.

I'm guessing that's an invitation for me to help him. I take the other end of the coiled tube and try cutting it with the box cutter. The blade is so dull that I have to use it like a breadknife, sawing through it in furious strokes, leaving the ends jagged and rough. For every one piece I cut, Hector is able to cut fifteen. But I don't want to push myself to cut too quickly. I could easily slice open the gloves of my suit if I'm not careful.

As I cut the tubes with Hector, still baffled over why we're doing this or why we couldn't have done it outside of the monster's abdomen, not speaking a word to each other, the sound of machine engines roar to life. The guy on the driller drives the machine directly into the wall of intestine. The drill spins, slicing the meat open. The tubes of intestine are massive, each one the size of a subway tunnel. As the driller opens up the thick fleshy wall, a flood of black goo spills out on top of him, soaking his suit in foul slop. But he doesn't stop pushing forward, cutting into the intestines like he's digging a tunnel through a mountain. Behind him, Hoji works the grinder, pulverizing the intestines into ground beef and spraying it out the back. Within minutes, Hoji is also covered in rot and gore. I realize now why he was pissed when Meri assigned him to work the grinder. He'll probably spend the whole day bathing in that putrid bacteria-ridden sludge.

Once Hector gets close to the end of the rubber tube, he yanks it out of my hand so that he can finish the job on his own. I just step back and nod in agreement, then put the box cutter back in the safe room.

A beeping noise echoes within the cavity as I return to Hector. The noise issues from a small buggy that pulls backward down the slope toward Meri. She waves to the driver, signaling for him to back it up closer to the mound of monster guts piling up behind the grinder. The cab of the buggy is sealed up. The driver within must be somebody from Waste Disposal, like the guy who brought me to the site in the dump truck. He wears a normal uniform, rather than a yellow rubber suit. It looks like he's in a hurry to get out of here. The buggy hauls a series of dumpster-sized carts, nine in total. Once he's backed far enough into the cavity, Meri unlatches the carts from the buggy and the driver speeds away, charging up the slope and into the tunnel as fast as the little vehicle can take him.

Meri notices me watching her and waves me over.

"Maggot, grab a shovel," she says to me. "You're on shit-tossing duty."

I nod and run back into the safe room, grab a shovel, and go to the carts. Bill and Sanchez are already there, shovels in their hands.

"Your job is easy," she tells me. "Whatever the grinder spits out, you shovel into these bins." She unlatches one of the carts and rolls it toward me. "All nine of them need to be

44

filled by the time Disposal comes back for them. You've got about an hour."

When I look at the carts, I panic. They are each the size of dumpsters. How am I supposed to fill nine dumpsters in the span of one hour?

As Meri walks away, she says, "Stay out of everyone's way. Watch out for worms. You should be fine." Then she turns and goes on to her own duties.

I look at the shovel in my hand, then at the pile of shredded intestine, then at the nine bins I need to fill. I'm beginning to realize that the fear of working inside of a giant monster's corpse isn't going to be the hardest part of this job. The hardest part is going to be the fact that I'm a one-hundred-and-forty-pound weakling who has never done a hard day's worth of work in my entire life. It'll be a miracle if I'm still standing by lunchtime.

I scoop a shovelful of black goop and toss it into my cart. Half of it slides off the shovel before it goes in. I have no idea how I'm going to get all of this shit inside of the bins within an hour. Bill and Sanchez are nearby, shoveling alongside me, so at least I don't have to do all the work myself. But still, I'm only getting about two cups of slop into the bin per scoop. Sanchez is able to get five times that with each attempt. Bill gets a little less per scoop, but he moves fast for an old guy and fills his bin faster than Sanchez and I combined.

It seems like an incredibly inefficient why to clear out this mess. No wonder it's taking them so long to remove the monster corpse from the city. At this rate, it's going to be years before the thing is completely cleaned away.

"Worms," Sanchez calls out, loud enough to be heard over the roars of the grinder.

I pause mid-scoop and look at his section of the mound. Five squirming tack worms roll around in the muck, hissing and barking at him. Bill comes to him with the bucket of tubes I cut up with Hector. The old guy digs his goo-smeared gloves into the bucket and pulls out a handful of the tubes. Then he tosses them at the worms.

"What does that do?" I ask, still curious about the function of the tubing I'd been responsible for cutting.

Before they explain it to me, I see why. The worms go for the tubes like some kind of prey. They slurp the tubes into their hook-toothed mouths and chew on them. Once a worm takes one of them down, Sanchez scoops it up with his shovel and drops it into the bin.

"Can't bite with their jaws stuffed with rubber," Sanchez tells me. He picks up another worm. It isn't moving anymore. It looks dead. "They choke on them."

I nod, finally understanding. It still seems like an odd way to handle the oversized parasites. Why don't they just kill them with the blade of their shovels?

Going back to shoveling, I watch the mound carefully for movement, making sure to keep my feet clear of any possible depth the worms might be lurking. After three scoops, I decide to grab a handful of tubes from the bucket near Bill and sprinkle them in the area near my feet. Just in case one of them comes at me when I'm not looking, they'll hopefully go for the tubes rather than my ankles. I don't know if it'll actually work but it makes me feel a bit more at ease.

As I dig deeper into the guts, I notice a piece too big for the shovel. It's long and looks kind of like a stick. At first, I think it's one of the worms, but it's much thinner and isn't moving. I decide to just pick it up with my glove. I noticed

Bill lifting up pieces with his hands from time to time, so I assume it's safe.

Examining the object closer, I wonder what the heck it could be. Beneath the sludge, it's white and hard. Finger bones poke out of the black goo on one end.

"What the fuck!" I cry, realizing I'm holding the remains of a human arm.

Sanchez looks at me, oddly concerned, "What's wrong?"

I point at the bones. "It's a fucking arm!"

The Hispanic guy laughs at me and keeps shoveling. "Yeah, there's a lot of those."

"But why? Where did it come from?"

"We're in the intestines," he says, nodding toward the walls. "What do you think the creature ate? There's thousands of dead bodies buried here."

"Are you serious?" I cry.

He nods. "Get used to it."

I look at the arm, then back at my coworker. "What do I do with it?"

"Toss it in the bin," he says.

"That's it? Shouldn't they be taken somewhere? Shouldn't the bodies be buried or brought back to their family members?"

He shakes his head. "They told us just to throw them away. Everything here gets incinerated."

"Seriously?"

He doesn't answer.

I look down at the bone. It seems cold just to toss it in the bin. This never would have been acceptable in the world before the creature. I wonder if people outside the city even know about this practice. Perhaps nobody wants to know. If their family was eaten they probably assume that was the end of them. I wonder if all the piles of shit the monster defecated across the country are also full of bones. I wonder what they've done with those remains. Perhaps they were just incinerated as well. Perhaps people don't want to see the remains of their family members after they've been digested and shit out like watermelon seeds.

I wonder if my parents' bodies are rotting in these guts somewhere. My parents, my friends, my neighbors—a lot of people I knew were eaten by this monster. Their bones have to still be in the digestive system. They were among the last humans to be consumed, so they wouldn't have been excreted before the monster was taken down.

As I drop the arm into the bin, I wonder if it was somebody I knew. The old lady that worked at the store down the road. The fat kid who bullied me when I was a freshman in high school. It could have belonged to anyone.

That's the real horror of working inside of the monster's guts. The place is one big festering graveyard.

The Waste Disposal guy returns with nine new carts, but I haven't even completed filling my first bin yet. Bill and Sanchez filled the other eight bins, however, so Meri isn't upset with me. She might not even realize the bin I was working on was the first one she gave me.

I spend the next hour shoveling as fast as I can but I'm still only able to fill one and a half bins while Sanchez and Bill tackle three or four. At the start of my fourth bin for the day, I'm exhausted. My back is sore. My legs wobble. My arms can barely hold the shovel. I can't even breathe in the gas mask, feeling so claustrophobic I want to rip it off and respire without it, even though the gaseous atmosphere in here would likely kill me within minutes.

All I'm doing is shoveling, yet it's still the hardest work I've ever done in my life. The closest I've ever had to a job requiring manual labor was just washing cars or doing yard work for my dad. Nothing like this.

One thing is for certain: if I'm going to be able to keep this job, I need to get into better shape.

At lunch time, we all go into the safe room, shower off all the crap on our suits and close the door. The room fills with breathable oxygen. When I take off my mask, I've never inhaled such rancid air in my life, but it's still a relief to go without the mask for a while.

We don't eat normal food for lunch. The risk of contamination is way too high. Instead, we eat packages of protein goo, sucking the contents out with a straw. The stuff tastes terrible but it feels so good to get real nutrients into my body. Since they cut rations last week, all I've head to eat has been old Christmas candy I found in a box in the garage of the house I've been squatting in. It's nice to eat something other than sugar, but the food hits my system hard. I feel dizzy. I guess I didn't realize how malnourished I've been as of late.

"You didn't die yet, Maggot," says Sanchez, sitting down in the chair next to me. "Good job."

He grabs my shoulder and squeezes it so hard that I can't tell if he's fiercely congratulating me or trying to hurt me. Either way, my aching muscles cringe at the embrace.

"Good job?" Bill asks him. "He hardly did shit. We're going to have to work double time to pick up his slack."

Sanchez shrugs. "He didn't run away or get himself killed yet, so he's doing way better than I expected he would."

"You expected to do his job for him?"

Sanchez shrugs again. "He's helping a little bit. If you were his size you wouldn't be able to do any better."

The old guy grumbles and then says, "But he's getting paid the same as us. He should do the same amount of work."

"It's his first day," Sanchez says. "Ease off him."

I can't believe somebody is actually defending me. I wonder if Sanchez actually is a nice guy. He looks scary and intimidating, and his friendliness tends to feel faked, like he's just fucking with me and really hates me just as much as the rest of them. But after this, I wonder if he genuinely does care about my wellbeing. Maybe he feels sorry for me or can relate to what I'm going through. Maybe he remembers how much it sucks to be a maggot like me.

But just as I begin to warm up to the big guy, Sanchez looks at me and says, "Being a dick to him is only going to make you feel bad once he gets himself killed."

Then he smiles at me in such a sadistic way that it seems like he can't wait for that moment to come.

PART TWO
CLOCKING OUT

CHAPTER
THREE

Nobody expected the monster to come to Portland when it did. For weeks before it happened, we were in a panic. The Reaper was heading north up the California coast, hitting San Diego, Los Angeles, San Francisco, and then into Oregon. But it bypassed Portland completely, focusing instead on the small towns along the coast—Newport, Tillamook, Seaside, Astoria. After it went through Seattle and then crossed the Canadian border, we thought we were able to relax. We went to sleep that night feeling safe, as though we had a long time before we'd have to worry about our city getting attacked. We had no idea it was going to backtrack toward us in the middle of the night.

I was fast asleep in my bed when the monster landed. It dropped out of the sky with such impact that it was like a bomb had detonated in the center of the city. One moment, I was deep inside of pleasant dreams. In the next, I was thrown out of bed, into the air. The blast shattered the windows, split the ceiling in half, and pulled the paint right off of the walls.

My body went into shock the second I landed on my bedroom floor, the wind knocked from my lungs, my elbows scraped open on the carpet. I sat up, gasping, looking around the room, wondering what the heck just happened. Even though my mind wasn't fully conscious, it only took a second to figure out what was going on.

I got to my feet and went to the broken window. A cloud of dust blocked out the sky, covering the city in a blanket of ash as though a volcano had erupted downtown. Every house in the neighborhood suffered from blast damage. Walls cracked apart, garages collapsed into driveways, roof shingles peeled off like potato skins. All the car alarms rang out in the neighborhood. They were the only lights I could see outside. The rest of the city was black, suffering from a massive power outage.

I backed away from the window as rocks and debris rained down on the street outside, banging on rooftops and smashing car windshields. A toilet fell from the sky and shattered in our driveway. A pack of dogs ran down the road, barking and yelping as though fireworks were exploding around them.

I couldn't see the creature in the distance, but I could tell it was there. Through all the dust and smoke, I saw movement. Something massive stepping through the darkness. A black mountain drifting across the cityscape. The ground rumbled with every step it took, shaking the walls, knocking the lamp from my nightstand. My flat screen television fell from my dresser, screen-first onto a pile of laundry on the floor.

My mother's cries echoed down the hallway, yelling out for help. I staggered out of my bedroom, trying to keep my balance as the ground quaked around me. Half of the house was bent sideways, sinking into the earth as if a sinkhole had opened up beneath the living room.

"David! Kevin!" my mother shouted.

When I passed my brother's room, his furniture was knocked to the floor. His bed was covered in glass. His bong collection was shattered on the hardwood floor. David wasn't anywhere to be seen. I looked over the railing into the living room, but he wasn't down there either. If he'd been asleep on the couch, as he usually was at that time of night, he would have been crushed by a ceiling fan. Hopefully he was okay.

My mother continued screaming. "David! Help me!"

When I pushed open her bedroom door, I saw the ceiling had caved in. Both of my parents were pinned to their bed.

"Mom!" I called out.

I ran toward her. The floor rumbled, knocking me off balance. I tripped and fell onto a pile of plaster and shingles. Cold wind and rain hit the back of my neck. I looked up through the massive hole in the roof. The sky was a cloud of ash. I couldn't see the moon or stars. Dust and small bits of debris drifted into the room like snowfall.

"Kevin?" my mother cried out.

Her hand poked out from the debris, reaching out for me.

"Are you okay?" she asked, more concerned for me than her, even though she was the one buried under a mountain of rubble.

I grabbed her hand and squeezed it. "I'm fine. What happened?"

It was obvious what happened, but I didn't know what else to say.

"Where's David?" she asked.

I shook my head. "I don't know. He's not in his room. I don't think he came home tonight."

Then I remembered David had gone downtown to drink with some friends that night. I wondered if he was still there, right at ground zero when the creature landed. I wondered if he was still alive.

Tears pooled in my eyes as I pulled pieces of debris from the pile, trying to get my mother out. I didn't really like my brother. He'd always picked on me. He always made me feel like a wimp and tormented me every day when we were kids. But the thought of losing him put a wrench in my heart.

"Wake up," my mother cried. "Come on. Wake up!"

"What are you talking about?" I asked. It sounded like she was talking to herself. I wondered if she was hit in the head, not thinking straight.

"Your father," she said. "He's not moving."

"Dad?" I asked.

I pulled away pieces of plaster until I got to the mattress. The legs of the bed had collapsed, flattening it to the floor. There was a bare foot covered in white powder. It was my father's. I grabbed his ankle and felt for a pulse. A faint beating throbbed against my index figure.

"He's still alive," I told my mom. "He must be unconscious."

"I can't get to him," she said.

I pulled away enough debris to get my mother free. She stood up, her nightgown covered in plaster powder. Outside of a few cuts and scrapes, she seemed fine. She shook plaster from her hair and then immediately went to work alongside me, helping to dig out my father.

When the rumbling grew louder, the shaking more intense, we knew the creature was coming closer, heading toward our side of the city. We knew we didn't have time to save my father. We knew, to survive, we had to get out of there as soon as possible. We only had minutes to get out of town. But we didn't give up. My mother was too afraid to go on without him.

When we finally pulled my father out of the wreckage, he looked dead. His body was limp. The side of his head was bleeding.

My mom jumped on top of him, shaking his shoulders to get him up. When he didn't regain consciousness, she pushed air into his lungs and pushed on his chest. "Come on. Breathe, Jerry. Breathe!"

She pushed so hard on his ribs that it sounded like they were about to crack. He woke up, coughing, and pushed her away. He sat up, cringing against the edge of the filthy mattress, wearing only his underwear, coughing up plaster. He looked at us in almost an annoyed way, as though he blamed us for the collapsed ceiling.

"We have to go," my mother said, pulling him to his feet. "It's coming."

My father didn't acknowledge her words. He just got to his feet, wobbling across the floor. He had a concussion and didn't seem to be thinking straight. But he still seemed to know exactly what was going on and exactly what we had to do.

The ground shook so severely that we couldn't walk normally. My father had to crawl across the carpet. My mother leaned against my father's back. I balanced against the hallway railing. As we went for the stairs, my mother called out for David, even though I already told her he wasn't home.

My mother tried to ask my father about what we should do, where we should go, but we couldn't hear each other over the noises outside. Not only had the rumbling grown louder, there was also the sound of buildings crumbling and collapsing all around us. People were screaming. Cars raced through the streets and collided with each other. Planes and helicopters roared through the sky dropping missiles. We heard explosions, cracks, and fissures ripping through the ground. But the loudest noise was this bellowing screech that could only have come from the monster itself—a sound like a crying whale mixed with two bulldozers slamming into each other.

"You're going to have to drive," my mother said, throwing me the keys. She knew I didn't like to drive. I didn't even have a license. But there was no other choice. They were too injured. I had to be the one to drive us.

We didn't bother getting dressed or grabbing supplies. We just went in whatever attire we slept in. My mom in her nightgown, I in my t-shirt and boxers. My dad in his briefs. We didn't even stop to grab our shoes.

I led the way outside, pushing through a strong gust of wind. It wasn't a natural wind, not coming from the sky. It was the force of the monster's feet hitting the ground, each step like a small atomic detonation.

"Come on," I cried, racing toward the minivan.

I unlocked the driver's side door and got in the seat. My parents moved slowly, nearly crawling toward the van. That's when I realized both of them were in worse shape than I thought. My father was covered in blood that gushed down his chest and stomach. His arm also looked dislocated. It dangled on the side of him like a useless flap of meat. Even my mother was worse than she let on. She was limping, breathing hard like she was having a mild heart attack. I'm not sure if they were only pretending their wounds weren't so bad for my sake, so that I wouldn't worry, or maybe they'd just been in so much shock they hadn't noticed their true condition.

Putting the key in the ignition with shaky, twitchy fingers, I couldn't believe it was up to me to get them to safety. In their condition, they wouldn't be able to help or even give me guidance. I had to navigate us through the city, figure out the safest path, all on my own.

Looking at my hands on the steering wheel, losing my breath every time the ground rumbled, I had no idea how I was going to get us out of there. I hardly even knew how to drive. If David was there, he would've known what to do. He was the kind of guy who planned for these kinds of scenarios. He had a whole strategy laid out if The Reaper were to ever attack Portland. He also had strategies for what he'd do if zombies attacked, a meteor hit the earth, or if we had to survive in a post-nuclear apocalypse. Sure most of his plans were all bullshit scenarios he came up with when he was stoned, but at least he'd given it some thought. All I did, all my parents did, was just hope the creature never came. But the thing did come and we had no idea what to do.

When my mom and dad got into the vehicle, I slammed on the gas and rammed right into the garage door. I thought for sure I had put it in reverse instead of drive. My parents didn't say a word. They just moaned in agony and held each other, trying to attach each other's seatbelts.

I put the minivan in reverse and backed out of the driveway. The vehicle bounced up and down with the rumbling, making it impossible to steer correctly. But I didn't stop. I ran over the shattered toilet in the driveway, hoping it didn't pop a hole in the tires. Once I got into the road, I sped off, avoiding rubble and debris.

When I looked back through the rearview mirror, I saw the monster for the first time. It was too big to see much of it clearly—just a giant mass of black scales. Its tail wagged back and forth, creating small tornados off in the Hawthorne district. Its feet were larger than any skyscraper downtown, crushing whole neighborhood blocks with every step.

The thing was only a few miles away. We had to go at top speed if we hoped to get out of there in time. But there was no way to go faster than thirty. The neighborhood was littered with rubble, overturned cars, collapsed houses that spilled into the street like mudslides. Only a few blocks down the street, the route was impassable. A five-car collision clogged the intersection. It looked like it just happened. Smoke poured out of the engines. Bodies littered the road.

"Take Foster," my mother said.

A woman came out of one of the wrecked cars, blood dripping down her forehead, yelling, "Help us!"

She looked like a crazed meth head, holding a small arm in her hand. It looked like it might have belonged to a child, perhaps her child. She was too confused to realize the rest of the kid was no longer attached.

I was too disturbed to stop for her or let her in. I hit the gas and went in reverse, pulling away from the wreck. Another man came out from behind the smashed cars with a handgun. He shot two rounds at us, shattering the windshield with one. My mother screamed. I turned around and went for Foster. It meant we'd be going right into the monster's path, but the road was much wider, less likely to be clogged with rubble and smashed cars.

But the second I turned the corner, the right front wheel fell into a deep pothole. I hit the gas. The wheel spun, but we couldn't move. We were stuck.

The man with the gun came up alongside the van and knocked on the window with the barrel. He was a large white guy, probably owned one of the seedy meth labs that populated the neighborhood.

"Get the fuck out," he yelled, pointing his gun at me.

I didn't argue. The van wasn't going anywhere anyway. I stepped out with my arms in the air. The ground rumbled so fiercely that I fell into his chest. He fired a round that whizzed past my ear and broke through the passenger side window.

"Want to die, dumbass," he said, blaming me for wasting a bullet.

He grabbed me by the hair and threw me to the ground.

The meth head woman staggered into the passenger seat, cradling the child's arm like a purse. She rocked back and forth, mumbling, "Come on, come on…"

My mother helped my father out of the backseat and we ran as fast as we could, back to our street. Behind us, the sound of the engine roaring as the meth head hit the gas, the tire spinning in circles in the pot hole. They weren't going anywhere. When I looked back, I could see him screaming at his passenger and slamming his fists into the steering wheel. Then he glared at me as though he blamed me for getting the vehicle stuck, as if I did it on purpose just to fuck him over.

"We have to go back for mom's car," I said, leading them back home, back toward the creature.

"There's no time," my mother said. "It's out of gas anyway."

I shook my head, pushing forward. We moved so slowly. Not only were my parents slow from their injuries, but we all walked barefoot. The gritty debris-speckled street tore up the tender bottoms of our feet.

"There's got to be at least *some* gas," I said. "We'll get farther than we would on foot."

My mother stopped running. My father fell to his knees.

I looked back at them. My mother had tears in her eyes. She shook her head at me. "There's no time."

Then she nodded her head toward our house and I saw what she meant. The creature was only minutes away. Its massive right foot came crashing down on the houses at the end of the road. The impact created a shockwave that rippled down the street, throwing cars, debris, and a cloud of dust our way. We ducked down and blocked our eyes, but all three of us were thrown back, tossing us two mailboxes down. A Buick flew over my head and crashed into the garage behind us. The ground split apart, causing deep fissures in the asphalt.

When the dust settled and I opened my eyes, I couldn't see our house anymore. Everything on our block had been razed to the ground, leaving mounds of rubble and concrete. Hundreds of tentacles stretched from the creature's abdomen, searching through the rubble, sucking up the dead bodies buried within.

I went to my parents. They weren't killed in the blast, but they might as well have been. Both of them were hit by debris. My dad was struck in the chest by a large rock. His skin tore open, exposing a section of his ribcage. One side of his chest was caved in. His lungs were probably collapsed. He wasn't able to speak and could hardly breathe. He tried to get up once and then fell back to the ground. I could tell from the look in his eyes that he wasn't going to ever try again.

My mother was in slightly better condition, but wasn't having any easier time getting to her feet. A large metal pipe was impaled through her upper leg. She tried covering it up when I went to her, not wanting me to see it even though the piece of metal was far too large to hide. She just shook her head, looked over at her father and back at me, just shaking her head and trying to hold back her tears.

Neither of them was able to run. I thought about whether I should stay with them or leave and save myself. But there wasn't enough time to get away, especially if I was running barefoot. The second the creature took one more step, we would all be dead. Either crushed under foot or pulverized in the massive explosion. We had only minutes left to live.

I thought that was it. I thought I would die right there. Not knowing what else to do, I went to my mother and wrapped my arms around her. She couldn't hold back her tears after that, letting out a loud sobbing howl. Pushing her face into my chest, I could feel her tears soaking through my t-shirt, rolling down my chest.

But before the monster's tentacles were done feeding on the corpses on our block, a motorcycle's headlight shined on us. Its engine roared in our direction. I looked back, squinting my eyes at the light. When I saw who was riding it, I couldn't believe my eyes.

"David?" I yelled at him.

My brother pulled up alongside us and asked, "What the hell are you still doing here?"

My mother's face brightened when she saw her other son. She continued crying, but her tears of sorrow had become tears of joy.

I didn't answer David's question. I just asked, "Where'd you get the bike?"

He shook his head. "Don't ask."

Our mom interrupted us with her serious tone. The same tone she always gave David when she didn't have time for his bullshit.

She told him, "Take your brother and get out of here. Now."

David looked back at the monster hovering over us, trying to gauge how much time he had.

"I'm not leaving you," David said.

"You only have room for one more person," she said. "Take Kevin. Your father and I aren't going to make it."

"I can fit one more person." There was desperation in his

voice. "You can sit on the handlebars."

Our mother shook her head. "Don't be ridiculous. I'd only slow you down."

Gun shots echoed from down the street as the meth head ran toward us. He must have given up on the minivan when he saw David drive by on the motorcycle. He needed new transportation and this time he would kill to get it.

"There's no time," our mother said. "Go."

Bullets whizzed past us as the meth head came closer. But he was too frantic to aim properly.

"Get out of here!" she screamed.

There wasn't time for a proper goodbye. I got on the back of the motorcycle and David hit the gas. He turned the motorcycle around and accelerated at full force toward the guy with the gun.

"Take care of each other," she called out to us. Then she yelled something I thought must have been "I love you" but I couldn't quite hear over the roaring engine and the sound of gunfire.

The tweaker aimed at David's head as we drove toward him, waiting for us to get close enough to hit with his poor aim. But when he pulled the trigger, nothing happened. He was out of bullets. We rode past him and his crazed girlfriend, weaving through the five car collision at the intersection, and kept on going.

When I looked back, I only saw my mother for a second as she held my father's twitching hand, watching us as we made our escape. Then the monster's mountainous foot came down behind them, sending a shockwave through the neighborhood, disintegrating their bodies upon impact.

The meth head ran after us, yelling at us to stop. When the shockwave hit, he got caught in the blast. His body was thrown at us, tumbling in summersaults across the asphalt.

His head hit a piece of debris midair, taking a large chunk out of the side of his skull.

David held his bike steady when we were hit by the blast. It pushed us forward, moving us faster, but it didn't knock us down. I felt the wheels leave the ground for a few feet. I'm not sure if it was because of the shockwave or if we just hit a bump in the road. But we landed safely and kept going at full speed.

When the tentacles came in, I saw them scoop up the meth head's girlfriend, still wriggling in the air, still clutching the severed arm tightly, as she was slurped up into the tube of meat. Then other tentacles wiggled toward the position where I last saw my parents. I turned away before they reached them, not wanting to see the creature eat their dead bodies. I just looked ahead, watching the road and hugging David tightly as he weaved through the obstacles.

I burst into tears at the thought of losing my parents. For years, I loathed being their child. I couldn't wait until the day I could finally leave the house, move to the other side of the country and never come back. But at that moment, once my wish came true, once I knew I'd never see them again, I realized how much of an idiot I'd been. They were strict and overbearing, but they were far from horrible parents. If I had to do it all over again, I never would have left home or taken them for granted ever again.

CHAPTER
FOUR

The lunch break only made me weaker. After stopping for a while, my body aches even worse than before. My arms are dead. My legs can barely hold me up. I'm ready to go home and sleep for a week. But I have to at least try. Bill glares at me like he'll kick my ass if I don't pull my weight. I've never been so intimidated by such an old guy in my whole life.

So I give it my best shot. Shoveling the guts one scoop at a time, I try ignoring the pain. I don't worry about matching the others' speed. Even in my best condition I couldn't keep up. But I don't want to look like too much of a pathetic maggot, so I at least try. Instead of focusing on big scoops, I try smaller ones taking only a dozen ounces of meat at a time. This way I'm at least able to appear as though I'm doing something, even though my bin doesn't fill very quickly. I'll be lucky to fill it halfway before Waste Disposal comes to pick it up.

My attempt at trying to look like I'm putting in the effort is enough to satisfy Bill and Sanchez. They obviously aren't happy with my progress, but they can't complain when they see me trying. But when Meri comes by to inspect our progress, it's another story.

She looks in my bin and sees that it's barely a quarter of the way filled.

"Is this your second or third bin?" she asks me.

I look at her glaring eyes through her mask and immediately stutter, not sure whether I should lie or tell the truth. I say, "I, uh… Yeah…" Then look away and pretend I didn't hear her. I go back to shoveling and hope that she'll lose interest and leave me alone.

"That's still his first one," Bill says.

Meri's eyes turn red. She looks like she's going to rip my throat out.

"Are you fucking kidding me?" she yells.

She grabs the shovel out of my hands so that I will pay attention to her.

"You can't even toss shit?" she asks. "If you can't even do this job then you're useless to me."

I don't know what to say. There's no excuse I can give that doesn't make me come across as even more pathetic.

"Look," she says, scooping chunks of meat into the bin. "How hard is this? Any idiot can use a shovel."

Within only a few minutes, she's able to do twice the work I was able to do in an hour.

"Is this really too hard for you?" she asks.

She hands me the shovel.

"Now you do it," she says.

I take the shovel and try to do it as she did, but I'm so nervous, so weak and sore, that I perform worse than I had done all day. Every scoop I take falls off of the shovel, landing on the side of the bin. I take four scoops but only get a couple of ounces of meat inside.

Meri staggers back, clutching the side of her mask as though the sight of my incompetence is literally sending a shock through her system. "Are you fucking serious? Is this really all you're capable of?"

She looks at the others. "Is this how he's been working all day?"

Sanchez chuckles and says, "Pretty much."

Bill chimes in. "Actually, he usually does even worse."

I can't believe they said that. They both saw me doing better than this earlier in the day. I can't believe they'd make that up just to get me in even more trouble.

"You're done," she says to me, taking the shovel from my hands. "Get out of my sight."

"Am I fired?" I ask, almost excited by the thought of it.

"If it were up to me you would be," she says. "Go clean up the safe room or something. Just stay out of my sight. In the morning, I want you to tell Frank that you can't handle this job. Make him transfer you to another crew. Whatever happens, I don't want to see you back here tomorrow. Got that?"

I am about to say *yeah*, but before I open my mouth she turns back to the mound of meat soup and begins to do my job for me. With how quickly she can shovel, she's bound to fill all the bins within half an hour.

I go back to the safe room and just sit down in a chair. I don't think I'll be able to get up anytime soon. Meri told me to clean up the place, but I don't know how I'm supposed to accomplish that task. There aren't any cleaning supplies in sight. There's a closed metal case in the corner of the room that could possibly contain a mop or broom, but I decide to wait for a while and check it out later. I've still got several hours before my shift ends. I'll have plenty of time to clean later. Or maybe I won't bother. I couldn't possibly piss off Meri more than I already have. Besides, I'll probably just fuck it up anyway.

After an hour of sitting there, the seat begins to hurt my

tailbone. I'm too weak to even sit in a chair. I just want to lie down on the floor and take a nap. But upon looking at the sight of the ground, all covered in meat and gore tracked in from the creature's guts, I decide not to.

Not sure what else to do, I go to the metal case to look for cleaning supplies, but the case is locked. I wonder if I should ask Meri for the keys, but quickly realize that would be the worst thing I could do. She wants me out of her sight. She would probably prefer I do nothing than have to deal with me again. So that's what I do: nothing. It's the only thing I'm competent at doing on this job.

There's a loud crashing sound outside the safe house. Then a commotion of shouts and yelling. Something's going on out there. I go to the safe house door to see what's going on.

"Traffic jam," someone shouts.

Another person repeats, "Traffic jam. Hoji, get out of there."

I don't know what they're talking about at first, but then I see it: there's a pile of cars at the other end of the cavity, spilling out of a large intestine. All of them crinkled and crushed, stripped of paint. All of the vehicles must have been swallowed by the creature and have been rotting in its guts this whole time. Some of them still contain the bones of their long digested passengers.

"Just great," Meri groans. "This is *exactly* what I needed today."

She puts her walkie-talkie to her mask and says "We've got traffic in here. Send in a tow."

I can hear the voice on the other end ask, "How many?"

Meri moves in closer. "I see at least seven, but there's probably even more up there ready to come out."

The person on the other end confirms the number and says some things I can't understand from my distance. Whatever it is, it ends the conversation.

Meri puts away her walkie and goes to her crew. "Hector, Mitch, we need to get the rest of the turds out of there so they can come pick them up. Climb up and tell me what we're dealing with, would ya?"

The two men nod their heads, but don't look too excited about the job she just gave them. Mitch goes up first, climbing up the stack of shit-covered vehicles. He moves slowly, taking careful steps. I'm thankful that isn't my job. The big bald guy climbs right up inside of the intestines, pushing large worms out of his way like they're as harmless as pesky lap dogs. Hector goes up behind him, but doesn't go all the way inside. He just waits at the top of the pile of vehicles, at the edge of the intestinal opening, maybe just acting as a liaison between Mitch and Meri.

The cars begin to rumble and shake like they're getting ready to fall over. Hector freezes in place, hugging himself tightly against the hood of a BMW. I hold my breath at the sight. If one of those vehicles comes loose, the whole stack could tumble over and crush him. Meri notices the danger as well, but doesn't call him down.

"Bill, Sanchez, get the hell out of there," she says to the two workers at the bottom of the pile.

The two men with shovels didn't stop working after the cars fell. They continue tossing chunks of meat into the bins, probably digging up the support that is holding up the stack of vehicles.

"Take a break," Meri tells them.

She doesn't have to tell them twice. Sanchez and Bill toss their shovels aside and head toward the safe room, toward me.

"Hoji, you too," she says to the Samoan, who was just about to get the grinder going again. "Get out of here."

Hoji gets off the grinder and goes to the safe room, pushing past me as he enters. Sanchez and Bill wait by me, watching the workers up inside the intestine. I wonder if this happens often. I couldn't imagine having to dig vehicles out of the creature's guts like this.

When Sanchez sees me standing next to him, he grabs me by the shoulder and squeezes in his painfully friendly way.

"Sorry about selling you out back there, Maggot," he says. At first I don't know what he's talking about, but then I realize he's referring to when he and Bill told Meri what a terrible job I was doing all day. "But I was doing you a favor. Getting kicked off of gut crew is the only way you're going to live. This job is way too dangerous for you."

I push his hand away, trying to focus on what's going on with the vehicles.

"There's something up there," Hector yells down to Meri. "Something *big*."

I look at Sanchez and ask, "Why is this job so dangerous, anyway? All I had to do was shovel shit and watch out for worms. It's really not that bad."

Behind me, Meri yells up at Hector.

"What is it?" she asks.

"Can't tell yet," Hector says.

Sanchez shakes his head at me. "That's the easy work. There's a whole lot of things on this job that can kill you. Especially when it comes to accidents. One false move here and you're as dead as being hit by a bus."

"Holy shit..." Hector says. "There's a whole city bus up here."

Just as he says that, the stack of cars rumble again.

"Get out of there!" Meri yells.

"Hold on…" Hector says.

"Now!"

But it's too late. A car in the middle becomes loose and slips out of the stack, knocking the others down. Hector jumps into the air, landing in a mound of slushy meat. Meri runs to him and pulls him out of the way as more cars come tumbling out of the intestine, crashing against each other.

When the bus comes sliding out, we see Mitch dangling from the door, trying to get inside for protection. There's a screeching metal sound as the bus slams into the wreckage and falls over lengthwise, crushing the grinder beneath it. The workers run toward their friend trapped inside of the bus.

"Is he okay?" Sanchez asks.

But before they can get to him, we see another vehicle sliding out of the intestinal tube.

"What the hell is that?" Bill asks.

When it comes halfway out, I recognize it, but can't believe what I see.

"It's a fucking helicopter," Hoji says.

But it's not just any helicopter. It's an apache attack helicopter. The kind the military used for fighting the monster. And this one was still fully armed, most likely devoured before even a single missile could be fired.

We just watch as the helicopter falls out of the intestine. There's no time to do anything but pray. We don't jump for cover. We don't scream a warning.

Upon impact with the bus, one of the missiles is detonated. It causes a chain reaction. It ignites the other explosives on the helicopter, then the gas tanks of the surrounding vehicles, then the gaseous fumes emitted by the creature's guts.

Jake and Mitch are the first to be swallowed by the flames. Then Hector, as he tries to run to safety. Meri hits the deck in time, but Sanchez is hit with shrapnel. Standing just a few feet closer to the blast than I am, the large Hispanic man takes all the damage, unintentionally shielding me from the explosion. Hoji and Bill, hiding inside the safe room, are the only two who are completely free from danger.

But the explosion isn't the end of it. The gasses inside of the intestine catch fire and the flames burrow deep inside of the monster's corpse, causing explosions for miles across the meat mountain. The walls around us shake and quiver. Boulders of meat rain down on our heads.

"It's caving in," Meri shouts, getting to her feet. "Into the safe room!"

She runs toward Sanchez and tries to get him to his feet, but he's too heavy to lift on his own.

She looks at me and says, "Help me."

I do as she asks. I grab him by the other arm and together we drag his writhing body out of the cavity, into the safe room. Once we shut the door, I watch through the tiny porthole as the ceiling collapses on top of us, burying us under a mountain of rotten black meat.

Meri fills the room with oxygen, making it safe enough to take off our masks.

"Where's the others?" Hoji asks. Being in the safe room the whole time and not seeing what just went down, he didn't know Mitch, Jake and Hector were dead.

Meri doesn't answer his question, going toward Sanchez and Bill. The old guy is trying to help his wounded coworker, but he doesn't know what he's doing. He removes a large piece of shrapnel from his arm and blood comes gushing out in large spurts.

"What the hell are you doing?" she asks him. "Tie that off."

Bill just holds the wound as though trying to push the blood back inside.

"Do I look like a fucking doctor?" Bill asks.

Sanchez rips his mask off, breathing the fresh air and whines. "Do something you old motherfucker." There's almost a soft chuckle between his words. "I better not die because of you."

The old guy doesn't give him any sympathy points. "Blow it out your ear, Sanchez."

"Make a tourniquet," Meri says.

She grabs some rubber tubing from the counter and tosses it to Bill, who immediately wraps it around his coworker's upper arm, trying to cut off the circulation.

"Blow it out your ear?" Sanchez asks, making fun of the old guy's word choice. "What kind of comeback is that?"

Bill is too focused on what he's doing to say anything. No matter how tightly he ties the tourniquet, blood continues to shoot out of Sanchez's arm.

"You're not doing it right," Meri yells.

"I've got it as tight as I can," he says.

When I see the blood spraying out in spurts, I can tell what's going on. I decide to step forward and speak up.

"His artery is severed," I say. "You've got to reach in there and clamp it off."

Meri nods at me and turns to Bill. "Do it."

Bill looks at us as though we're crazy. "Are you fucking kidding me? You want me to do *what?*"

I run forward and push Bill aside. "Get out of my way. I'll do it."

Meri nods at the old guy, telling him to let me take over.

I have no idea what I'm doing, but I've seen enough medical shows to know this is exactly what needs to be done. And if somebody doesn't do it, Sanchez is definitely going to bleed to death.

"Are you seriously letting the maggot save my life?" Sanchez says, whining as I move toward him. He tries to laugh, but this time his laughter can't hide his anxiety. "Don't you think *anyone else* would do a better job?"

The wound is deep enough that I can fit three of my fingers inside. I just reach in, probe around and grab what feels like a tiny gooey tube. I'm not sure I've got the artery until I notice the blood has stopped flowing.

"God damn," Bill says. "The maggot did it. He's not bleeding anymore."

"We need something to clamp it down with," I tell them.

"Like what?" Meri asks.

"I don't know what you have," I say. "Anything that can hold a tube firmly shut. Preferably something small."

Meri goes for the metal case in the corner of the room, unlocks it, and digs through the supplies.

As I sit here, waiting for her to come back, feeling awkward with my fingers inside Sanchez's bulbous arm, the reality of the situation sets in. I can't believe I'm even attempting this. I don't even know if it's actually going to work. I look at Sanchez. He looks back at me and winks, as though totally aware of how uncomfortable this is for both of us.

"You're still wearing your gloves," Bill says, standing over my shoulder. "Shouldn't you have taken them off first?"

I shake my head. "There wasn't any time."

"But your gloves are all covered in shit," he says. "You've infected him. He's going to have to get his arm cut off now, dumb ass."

For a second, I think he's right. I'm an idiot for not taking my arm out of my suit before attempting this. But I shake the thought from my head. I did the right thing.

"It doesn't matter," I say. "The shrapnel that cut into

him already caused an infection. He was going to lose his arm either way."

Bill turns around and grumbles. "Well, I wouldn't have done it that way. I would've known better. He might not have been infected yet. Now he is for sure."

Sanchez waves his coworkers words away. "Bullshit, Bill. I almost bled to death thanks to you."

"Hey, fuck you, Sanchez," he yells, getting unreasonably defensive with the wounded man. "I should have just let you bleed."

I don't say it out loud, but Sanchez would have been much better off if Bill didn't try to help him. Bill removed the shrapnel that was stopping the blood flow. Removing it is why Sanchez is now in danger of bleeding to death. He should have just left it in place until we could have gotten him help.

"I bleed good, Billy," Sanchez says, laughing out loud. "I bleed good."

I have no idea what he's talking about. It sounds like he's getting delirious from the shock. Maybe there's not enough blood getting to his brain.

"I'm like a vampire," he says, giggling. "You want to fuck with a vampire?"

"Hurry up," I tell Meri. "He's getting delirious."

Bill shakes his head. "He's not getting delirious. He's always this weird."

Sanchez just chuckles. I have no idea what's going on with him anymore.

Meri returns and asks, "Will this work?"

She holds out a small clamping mechanism that looks somewhat like a metal clothes pin. I'm not sure what it's really used for.

I shake my head. "It's too big."

"It's the best I got," she says.

"We're going to have to cauterize it, then," I say.

"Can we do that with an artery?" she asks.

I shrug. "I assume so. We have to do something."

"What do you need?" she asks.

"Got a blowtorch or something?"

She shakes her head. "It's too dangerous to use flames down here. We don't even have a lighter."

I look around the room.

"Does the generator run on gasoline?" I ask.

She nods.

"Bring me some."

I unzip my rubber suit and pull my free arm out of the sleeve. Then I dig into my pants, searching for my lighter. Lucky for Sanchez I recently picked up smoking. Otherwise, I wouldn't have brought a lighter to work and he would've been screwed.

When Meri returns with a gallon of gasoline, I tell her, "Splash some of it into the wound."

"Oh, shit..." Bill says. He turns away. "I'm not watching this. This is going to be fucked up."

As Meri pours it in, I say, "Not too much. Just enough to catch fire. If you pour in too much then it will take too long to burn off." I look at Sanchez. "It'll just make it more painful."

"Aren't you going to pull your hand out?" Meri asks, as she pours the gas all over my glove as I hold my fingers inside of Sanchez's wound.

I shake my head. "Not until the last second."

"You got some guts, Maggot," Sanchez tells me, wincing at the pain of the gasoline burning his wound.

I don't thank him for the compliment. I just stare him in the eyes and tell him, "This is going to hurt. A lot."

"Has this ever happened to you before?" he asks.

I shake my head.

He smiles and says. "Then how do you know how much this is going to hurt?"

I shrug, bringing the lighter to his wound. "I've got a good imagination."

Then I set the gasoline on fire and pull my hand away. He shrieks as his wound bursts into flames. It's obvious we used too much gasoline. It should've just taken a second or two to burn off, but the flame goes for a full minute and a half.

Sanchez bangs his fist on the metal floor, screaming and cringing at the pain.

The whole wound is horribly burned by the time the flame finally goes out, but at least the bleeding stopped.

"Sorry," I tell him.

"Sorry for what?" Sanchez asks.

"I burned you too much. It's going to leave a horrible scar."

"Don't worry about the scar," he says. "I'll have to get my whole arm cut off anyway."

I nod at him, still in shock that my plan actually worked.

"It's okay, though." Sanchez chuckles through the lingering pain. "I still got another one."

Then he smacks me on the shoulder so hard it nearly knocks me to the ground. Even with all the blood loss, he still has the strength of an ox.

"What now?" Hoji asks. "When are they coming to get us?"

He had remained silent when Sanchez needed help, not offering even a finger of assistance. But he's not interested in staying quiet anymore. He wants answers.

Meri doesn't respond to him right away. She stares through the porthole on the door, the only window looking outside the safe room. She doesn't look at him or say a word. She just holds out her walkie-talkie and hits the button. There's only static on the other end.

"What the fuck is that supposed to mean?" he asks.

"I can't get through to anyone," Meri says. "That's what that means."

"Where the hell are they? Why aren't they picking up?"

Meri shakes her head. "We're buried under hundreds of thousands of tons of meat, not to mention a hide that's as strong as fifty-inch steel. If I can't get through to anyone that means the tunnel outside has collapsed. Our only way out is gone. We're stuck here."

"For how long?" Hoji asks.

She shrugs. "Until they dig us out."

"How long will that be?"

"About as long as it took them to dig this deep in the first place."

"And how long did that take?"

"Not long. A couple weeks or so."

"Two weeks?" Hoji yells. "We're going to be stuck here for two fucking weeks?"

"That's if they even have the manpower," she explains. "Who knows how big the explosion was in the rest of The Meat. It's possible it killed a large percentage of the workforce. It's possible they've got even bigger problems to deal with than us."

Hoji looks around the room, trying to find someone to blame, somebody to punch for putting him in this situation.

Bill asks, "How long can we stay down here?"

Meri shakes her head. "We've got a week's worth of food and water, but the oxygen isn't going to last more than a day."

"What the fuck are we going to do if our oxygen runs out?" Hoji asks.

Meri doesn't answer. She just looks through the porthole, even though there's nothing but meat on the other side.

"This is fucked," Hoji says, kicking over a chair. "This shit ain't never happened before." Then he looks at me. "You're bad luck, Maggot. Bad, bad fucking luck."

CHAPTER
FIVE

David and I roared down the street on the motorcycle, weaving through broken down vehicles and rubble. The major roads were packed with traffic. Cars were even pulled up on the sidewalks, trying to get around each other. But nobody was going anywhere. Who knows what was blocking traffic up ahead. Probably a pile of wrecked vehicles or a footprint that turned an intersection into a massive crater. But everyone still tried to use the road. Everyone still waited their turn, violently honking their horns at the cars ahead, as if the only person to blame for the traffic was the car immediately in front of them.

With our motorcycle, we didn't have to worry about the traffic. We could weave between the cars, ride around them. Everyone sneering and yelling at us as we passed them by, either due to anger for not waiting our turn or out of jealousy that they didn't have a motorcycle of their own.

"We need to keep an eye out around these people," David told me, as we sped through the traffic. "They're desperate. If you see anyone pull out a gun you let me know. We can't give up the motorcycle."

Three large guys that looked like football players stepped out of a frat boy pickup truck and pointed at us. They didn't have guns, but one had a crowbar and another had a baseball bat. They charged straight for us.

"Up ahead," I yelled at David.

He said, "I see them."

Then he weaved around the next car and hit the gas. We both ducked as a baseball bat swung over our heads, hitting the headlight of the Ford Taurus on our right. The others came up from behind, but weren't fast enough. David went up on the sidewalk and picked up momentum, leaving the assholes in our smoke. But then something hit me square in the back and I cried out in pain. When I heard the clanking on the street behind us, I realized that one of them had thrown his tire iron at us.

"You okay?" David asked.

The pain rippled through my back. I could hardly breathe. The wind was knocked from my lungs.

"I'll… be okay…" I said between gasps.

But I really wasn't in very good shape. I could already feel bruising and swelling on the back of my ribcage. That asshole who threw the tire iron didn't even do it to get the bike from us. He just wanted to hurt one of us, punishment for getting away from them.

Then I remember that the bike isn't even David's. I wonder what he did to get it. Was he the asshole in a different scenario? Did he hit someone with a tire iron and steal their bike? Or did he take from someone who was already dead? Or did a friend who didn't need it anymore give it to him? I thought about it for a while and realized that I really didn't know my brother like I thought I did. I didn't know what he was really capable of.

Farther down the road, we didn't have to worry about anyone stealing our bike. There wasn't anyone in sight. All the cars were abandoned. Hundreds of vehicles left empty like a parking lot in the middle of the street, headlights still shining, doors wide open. That was why the traffic jam was so bad behind us. All of the people in the cars ahead of us got sick of waiting for the traffic to pick up so they abandoned their vehicles and continued on foot. I had no idea where they all went. Did they continue forward or run in different directions? It was the same thing on all the side streets. The traffic was gridlocked everywhere we looked.

We kept on down the road, hoping we'd get around whatever obstacles got in our way. Without people around, we felt like we could relax, we felt like we could get out of town within the hour. But David saw something up ahead, a glowing light in the distance.

"Shit..." David said.

"What?" I asked.

"I should've known..." he said. "I'm so fucking stupid..."

"What's wrong?"

He didn't answer. He just kept driving toward the glowing light. Once we arrived, I saw what he was talking about. A massive trench filled with blue fire blocked the road. It stretched as far as we could see in every direction, all the way across the town.

"The Reaper's already blocked off this side of town," he said. "We're stuck."

He stopped the bike and we got off, looking at the pit of flames. "What do you mean? He did this on purpose to block us in?"

"Don't you watch the news?" David said. "This is what

85

he does. He breathes fire across the edges of the town to trap us all inside, so we can't get away. We're not going to be able to get out."

"What if we go east, toward Troutdale?" I asked.

He shook his head. "We can try, but I'm sure he blocked off all the exits already."

"Can't we go over it?" I asked.

David coughed a laugh. "How? Jump it with the motorcycle? Who do you think I am, Evel Knievel?"

I tried to think about it, but it didn't seem possible. I threw one idea out there, "If we can create a grappling hook somehow we can go from the roof of a building to a building on the other side."

"Trust me, it won't work," David said.

"What if we went to a fire station, got some fireproof firemen suits and walked through it?"

"Impossible."

"We could roll cars into the pit until it makes a bridge we could cross."

"Don't be ridiculous." David just laughed at my ideas and shook his head. "Those flames can melt steel in seconds. We can't even get through them on the river. The only way past is to fly over them, hundreds of feet up. I've seen videos of them catching low-flying helicopters on fire. Forget about crossing it."

I didn't have any other ideas, but it was hard to just accept it. We were so close to escaping. Safety was just on the other side. If we could only get across the flames we would be home free. But I believed David. He knew more than I did about The Reaper. I was sure he was right.

"Get on the bike," he said. "We should just keep moving. That thing is bound to leave town eventually. We just need to stay alive until it does."

"So we're just going to go back to town and hope for the best?" I asked.

"We just need to stay as far away from that thing as possible," he said. "Hundreds of people survive every monster attack. We just need to make sure we're one of the lucky ones."

I got onto the back of the bike and said, "I've never been very good with luck. Have you?"

"Nope." He snickered. "But maybe we've just been saving it all up for today."

We went west toward the Willamette River and entered an area that had already been destroyed by The Reaper.

"If we stay here we should be safe," David said. "The Reaper won't return to an area he's already cleared."

"Are you sure?" I asked.

David shrugged. "I'm just guessing, but it makes sense, right? He will likely focus on the parts of town he hasn't reached yet."

I looked across the wasteland of rubble. It didn't seem very safe. It was dark and treacherous. And my lack of clothes and shoes made it next to impossible to travel through without getting sliced up.

"But won't we have to abandon the bike?" I asked. "We can't drive it in there."

David looked down at the motorcycle dashboard. "We're low on gas anyway. We'd only be able to continue for another half hour. I think this is our best option."

I really didn't like the idea of abandoning the bike and going into the ruins. If the creature came through this area we wouldn't be able to move very quickly. Not just because we didn't have a vehicle but because there are no flat surfaces. We wouldn't even be able to run.

I shook my head. "I think we should wait. Stay at the edge of the ruins for now, stay with the bike. That way we can escape if it happens to return to the area."

David nodded. "Okay. Sounds like a decent compromise. We'll wait here for now."

We drove the bike beneath the roof of a half-collapsed warehouse, out of sight just in case anyone wanted to jack it from us. David broke into the Goodwill across the street and brought me back some clothes to wear: wool golfer pants, hiking boots, and a black trench coat. It was a vast improvement over going around in just boxers and a t-shirt for the rest of the night. We sat against the wall, under an overhang to protect us from the rain.

The creature was across town, stomping and eating everything in its path, spraying blue fire from its mouth at the planes and helicopters circling its head. We didn't let that thing out of our sight, keeping track of what it was doing, where it was headed, just in case we needed to get out of there in a hurry. The ground still rumbled with every step it took, but the tremors were mild enough to tolerate.

David lit up a joint and took a long drag.

"Are you sure you want to be stoned right now?" I asked him, rubbing the swelling lump on my back.

He laughed. "Hell yeah I do. No better time than right now."

"You'd be better off with a clear head."

He shook my words away with the smoke billowing out of his mouth. "After all the shit I've seen tonight, this is the only thing that'll keep me sane. Plus, for all I know, this might be the last joint I ever smoke. If I gotta go, I'd rather go enjoying myself."

I nodded. Couldn't disagree with that.

He offered me a hit of the joint. "Want some?"

I shook my head. "It'll just make me paranoid."

"Paranoid? This is good shit. It'll relax you. They call it Granddaddy Purple down at the dispensary."

Ever since they made recreational marijuana legal in Oregon, David had been their number one customer. He had already been a big pot smoker before that, but he really had a field day once it became legal. Our parents didn't approve of it, just as they didn't approve of smoking tobacco or drinking alcohol other than a glass of wine with dinner every now and then, but once it became legal they had no choice but to accept his habit. He was an adult. He had the right to do whatever he wanted as long as he didn't break the law.

"No," I said, waving it away. "I wish I had some vodka though. I'd kill for some vodka."

My brother laughed through his smoke. "You drink vodka? Straight or in cocktails?"

"Straight if it's good enough," I said. "I prefer potato vodka. Chopin if I can afford it."

"No shit..." David said. "You drink vodka straight? Nobody drinks vodka straight."

"Russians do. I do. It's the only liquor I can stand."

David shook his head. "I don't touch the stuff. If I'm drinking something hard it's bourbon every time."

"Bourbon makes me gag."

"You're drinking the wrong bourbon, little bro. I'll get you some that'll change your mind." He paused for a moment. "Someday."

It seemed like the first time I really ever hung out with my brother. We did everything together when we were kids. We hated each other, but we still did things. Played board games. Kicked the ball around the yard. Played Xbox. But not since we'd grown up. We didn't go to high school together. We didn't like any of the same bands. We never even drank together. David didn't even know I drank vodka.

"It's never going to be the same is it?" I asked him. "Even if we get out of this, we don't have a home anymore. We won't even have a hometown when The Reaper's through with it. And mom and dad..."

I couldn't finish my words. My throat swelled up. I tried not to think about it. I couldn't believe they were gone.

David wrapped his arm around my shoulder. "Don't worry. No matter what happens, we'll still be together." He took another hit and exhaled. "I've been a shitty brother. I've never been there for you. That's all going to change. I promise you that. Once this is over, I'll be there for you."

I shook my head. "You already have been there for me. If it wasn't for you I'd have died back there. You saved my life."

David smirked. "Well, I thought about leaving town without going back home. But I couldn't do it. I didn't think you'd still be there. I didn't know I would end up saving your life. But I couldn't leave town without knowing whether you got out or not. If I escaped and never heard from you or mom or dad I don't know what I'd do. I'd spend the rest of my life regretting it, wondering what would have happened had I gone back. Even if the house was demolished and you were all dead, at least I'd know for sure."

I nodded. I couldn't imagine being in his position. I wasn't sure I would have done the same thing. I probably would have been too afraid to charge right into the monster's path just to see if my family was okay. My brother would probably have been killed if the situation was reversed.

"Well, I'm glad you came back," I said. "I'll have to make it up to you someday."

While sitting on the corner, a VW Bus drove casually down the road. It pulled up to the curb, right in front of us. A hippie couple sat in the front seat, smoking weed and listening to a Sly and the Family Stone cassette tape on their old stereo system.

"How's it going, bros?" the driver asked, lowering his sunglasses.

My brother and I looked at each other. They were so casual, so out of place. It was like they didn't even realize what was going on around them.

"Hey," David said.

The girl in the passenger seat, wearing a flowery headband, smiled at us. She chewed gum between puffs of weed.

"You guys seem like you're in some trouble out here. You need a lift?"'

David and I just laughed. We didn't know what else to do.

"No, we're good," David said.

"You sure?" the hippie asked. "It's pretty dangerous out here. I don't know if you've noticed, but there's some bigass monster out here eating the whole city."

David snickered. "Yeah, I've noticed."

The hippies snickered with him, realizing the absurdity of their statement. I couldn't tell if they were joking or baked out of their minds.

"Well, we're going to try to get out of town," the hippie said. "There's an artist commune over in the gorge that's supposed to be pretty safe. My brother went out there last week. Wish we would have gone with him when we had the chance."

David shook his head at the hippies. "I hate to break it to you, but all the roads out of town are cut off. There's no way out."

The hippie's eyes widened like my brother just blew his mind. "Seriously? Are you sure about that?"

David nodded. "We just tried to get out on the south side. It's a dead end. The bridges are destroyed, so you can't go over the river to the west. I don't know about the east or north. You can try it but I'm sure it's the same thing. Best thing to do is hide and wait it out."

The hippie thought about it for a minute. "Think we'll still go for the 84 and hope for the best."

"Are you sure?"

The hippie shrugged. "I've got a good feeling about it. Everything goes your way if you keep a positive state of mind, brother."

"Well, good luck," David said.

"You, too, my man," said the hippie. "Peace out."

Then they rolled up their windows and drove on. We watched them slowly roll down the street, cruising down the road like they had all the time in the world. They even used their turn signal at the next stop sign.

Once they were out of sight, David and I looked at each other.

"What the fuck was that?" I asked.

David shrugged and said, "Just a couple of hippies driving through the apocalypse, I guess."

Then we laughed.

We were only safe for another forty minutes. The monster switched directions and was on a path heading back toward our location.

"We've got to clear out," David said. "What should we do?

Go into the ruins on foot or take the motorcycle as far as the gas can get us?"

Based on the trajectory of the monster's path, there was only one option left.

"The motorcycle," I said.

"Are you sure?"

I pointed at the creature. "Unless it changes directions, it's going to go right through the ruins. We're better off going somewhere else. Maybe we can find another destroyed neighborhood we can hide in."

David agreed. "Okay, let's go."

The rumbling ground was getting more intense as we went into the dilapidated warehouse for the motorcycle. I had to hold on to the walls to balance myself.

David rolled the bike around, facing the exit. Then he turned the key. There was a sputtering sound, but it didn't start.

"What's wrong?" I asked.

He tried again. Nothing.

"I don't know," he said.

"Can you fix it?" I asked.

"I don't know anything about motorcycles," he said in an aggravated tone.

He kept trying but it wouldn't work. I wondered if the rumbling tremors knocked something loose. Or maybe we were already out of gas and didn't know it yet.

"We have to go on foot," I said.

"We'll never outrun it," David said, attempting to start the bike one last time.

"Well, we can't stay here," I said.

"Let's go into the ruins," David said. "I still think it's the safest place."

"But he's heading right for them," I said.

"He'll change direction," David said. "I'm sure he will. He's already covered that area. He doesn't need to go there again."

"Unless he's passing through, crossing the river to get to Tigard and Beaverton. I doubt he's hit those areas yet."

The rumbling hit harder, shaking the building. Plaster and debris rained down on us from the ceiling.

"Let's get out of here," David said.

We abandoned the vehicle and went for the ruins. We knew there was a good chance it wasn't safe, but it was slightly safer than heading to the neighborhood to the southeast, a neighborhood the creature hadn't gotten to yet. That place would surely be an all you can eat buffet for the monster, whereas the ruins would be like three-day-old leftovers sitting at the bottom of the refrigerator. We hoped the monster wouldn't choose the leftovers, even though he was heading in that direction.

Moving through the ruined section of the city wasn't easy. Even though I had boots and more protective clothing now, it was still too dark to see anything and the rain made it too slippery to climb through.

The Reaper didn't seem like it was going to switch course. It kept coming our way. If it stepped down anywhere near us that would be it. We'd be dead. We moved as quickly as we could, constantly tripping and falling on debris. I banged my chin so hard that blood gushed down my neck.

"Keep going," David yelled, ten yards ahead of me. "We can make it."

But I had no idea how we were going to get out of the

creature's path. It would be able to catch up in no time. Even though we tried going south through the wreckage, trying to get out of its path, there just was no way. We just had to pray it changed directions. The only way to make it was if it changed directions. But it didn't seem like that was going to be the case.

I slipped between two slabs of concrete and fell face-first into a cylinder of metal. It must have been a toppled street light or metal telephone pole. I couldn't tell in the dark. I spit out blood and a broken tooth, then tried to get back up. But I couldn't move. My leg was stuck. I pulled at it, pushing on the debris that pinned me down with my free foot. But it wouldn't budge. I couldn't get out.

In the panic, I only got myself more stuck. I slipped off of the concrete slab that held me up and landed in an awkward position, too crooked to lift myself up.

"David!" I cried. "Help me out!"

I didn't know what else to do but get his help. I couldn't even get myself upright anymore, twisted at such an odd angle.

He came running back for me. "What's wrong?"

"I'm stuck," I said. "Help me out of this."

He jumped down the concrete slab and grabbed my leg, trying to yank it out as quickly as possible. But it wouldn't budge for him either.

"Fuck..." he said.

He tried again but couldn't get me free.

"Keep going," I told him. "Forget about me."

"Fuck that," he said. "I had to leave mom and dad. I'm not leaving you."

"Seriously," David said. "I'm not going anywhere."

"Then you're going to die."

He shook his head. "No, we're both just going to wait

here. The Reaper will change directions. You'll see."

We sat there, watching the creature as it came closer. It didn't look like it would change directions. David was wrong.

But then something hit the beast in the back of the head and it roared in pain. We looked to the east and saw five fighter jets flying in. They were like nothing I'd ever seen. A new type of aircraft the military must have just recently developed. They launched strange cone-shaped missiles at the beast from every direction, hitting it in multiple places on its upper body. Like all previous attempts, the missiles couldn't penetrate its thick hide. But these missiles were different. They attached themselves to the outside of the creature's husk and drilled their way inside.

The creature tried to swipe them off, but the missiles hit in precise locations where it couldn't reach. The missiles drilled into it at a slow pace, but were able to penetrate the hide.

We just watched with bated breaths, wondering what was happening. The creature's shrieks echoed across the city, so piercing that we had to cover our ears even though it was miles away.

A few minutes of drilling, smoke and flames spraying out of the holes in the creature's neck. Then the bombs were detonated and the explosion opened massive holes in the monster's torso. Its neck ripped open, its head severed from its spine. It swayed up there for a moment as the light left its eyes. Then it collapsed.

The impact of its fall sent shockwaves across the city. David and I ducked for cover, holding each other behind that concrete slab as debris flew overhead. When it was all over and the dust cleared from the sky, we stared at the massive body spread across the length of Portland.

"Holy shit…" David said. "They actually did it."

I nodded in agreement. I couldn't believe it either.

"Is it dead?" I asked. "Is it really dead this time?"

We waited there for what felt like hours, waiting for it to get up. But it stayed down. David finally freed my leg and we crawled our way out of the ruins just as the sun started to come up. Military helicopters came in, circling the creature. They fired more missiles at it. Three more waves of them. Just to make sure it was dead.

David and I just watched from a distance, smiling and cheering. We broke into a nearby liquor store and took a bottle of vodka and bottle of bourbon. Then we drank ourselves stupid in the street, celebrating the death of the creature we called The Reaper.

"The Reaper's dead!" we cried. "The Reaper's dead!"

Every survivor we came across celebrated with us, taking swigs from our bottles, jumping up and down with excitement. We beat the thing. We finally beat it. Even though we lost so many people, so many loved ones. Even though half our country was in ruins. We had destroyed the beast. We had fought off the apocalypse.

No victory in the history of mankind had ever tasted sweeter.

CHAPTER
SIX

We wait for hours, but there's no sign of rescue. Meri clutches the walkie, checking it every five minutes, hoping to hear someone on the other end. But there's only static.

"Where the fuck are they?" Hoji complains, pacing around the room. He's the angriest and most nervous of us. His anxiety keeps us all on edge. "I'm not spending the night in this shithole."

"I think they opened a new Motel 6 in the monster's butthole," Sanchez says to him, giggling so hard it causes him to cringe in pain. "You can stay there if this room isn't good enough for you."

Hoji looks at Sanchez as though he will kick him in the stomach. If Sanchez wasn't so wounded, he probably would have.

"Fuck you, Sanchez," is all Hoji can say in response.

Meri does nothing to break up the bickering. She sits by herself, holding the walkie tightly, lost in thought. She looks worried. It seems out of character for her. She doesn't seem to be the kind of person who ever gets worried about anything. I assumed that's why she was put in charge of gut crew. More than any of the older more experienced workers, she could handle anything thrown her way. But this is new. She's probably never been in a situation like this before.

Bill presses his ear to the wall. "I don't hear any drilling. Shouldn't I hear drilling?"

Meri looks over at him. "Yeah, if they were working on a rescue."

"You don't think they plan to rescue us?" he asks.

Meri shrugs. "It would be a lot easier just to leave us down here and get a replacement team. It's not like they can't get away with it. There's no one holding them accountable. People die on this job all the time. We're all disposable."

For being the person responsible for holding her team together, Meri's not doing that great of a job. Her words send the men into a panic, making them even more stressed and anxious than they had already been.

"Bullshit," Bill says. "They're not going to do that. Frank's an asshole, but he's not *that* big of an asshole."

"It's not Frank's call to make," Meri says. "His bosses never met us, so they don't give a shit about us. They won't have any problem leaving us to die if the resources to rescue us are better used elsewhere. All they care about is meeting their contracted deadline."

"But when the media hears about this…" Bill begins.

"What media?" she says. "There's no media in Portland anymore. And with the quarantine up, there's no outside media that can get in."

"So we just wait here and hope they come?" Bill asks.

Meri pauses, looks away from him, then she shakes her head. "We can't stay here."

"What?" Bill cries. "Why the hell not?"

She points up at the ceiling. We all look. The corners are wrinkled, the center sags downward, and cracks are forming at the base of the walls.

"We don't have to worry about running out of oxygen," Meri says. "We don't have to worry about starving or dying of thirst. If we stay in here for much longer we'll be crushed to death."

We all stand up and look around the room. She's right. The ceiling looks like it could give away at any minute.

Meri adds, "Besides, Sanchez will die if we don't get him to a doctor."

Hoji charges Meri like he's about to strangle her. But once she turns to him and looks him in the eyes with her *don't fuck with me* face, Hoji immediately halts his assault.

Instead, he yells at her, "And how the hell do we do that? We dig our way out?"

She nods. "If we can dig our way to the driller we can burrow our way out."

Bill asks, "But wouldn't that still take weeks?"

"Not if someone out there drills from the other side. It will cut the time in half."

"That's *if* they plan to rescue us," Hoji says.

Meri says, "Once we start drilling, they'll likely hear us on the other side. They'll know we're still alive. I'm sure they'll do everything they can to get us out then. We might even be able to communicate with them once we drill far enough."

There's a new light of hope in everyone's eyes. But only for a second. Only until Sanchez opens his mouth.

"Sorry, Chief," Sanchez says. "It's a good plan but it's not going to work."

"Why's that?" Meri asks.

"The driller was destroyed in the blast," he says.

"How the fuck do you know that?" Hoji asks.

Sanchez lifts the piece of shrapnel Bill pulled out of his arm and tosses it toward us. "Because a piece of it nearly killed me."

All hope slips out of everyone's eyes and Hoji flips a table over. The crashing noise echoes through the tiny ever-shrinking room.

"Then that's it," Meri says. "That's the only option we had left."

She sits down in a chair and leans back, letting out a long exhale, ready to just give up and die.

"Not necessarily," I say.

They look at me as though they forgot I was even in the room with them, surprised I would dare to speak up at a time like this.

"*You've* got an idea?" Bill asks, then he smirks in a condescending way, like a dumb maggot like me couldn't possibly add anything to the conversation.

I suddenly feel nervous giving them my thoughts. When I speak, my words don't come out properly.

I say, "Well, if we can't make a tunnel, can't we just take one that already exists?"

Bill points in my face as he yells, "All the tunnels have collapsed, dumbass. Aren't you paying attention?"

I shake my head. "Not the manmade tunnels. I mean the natural ones."

They look at me with blank stares. They obviously have no idea what I'm talking about.

I explain, "We're in the monster's digestive system, right? The whole digestive system is just one big tunnel. Can't we just walk through it and get out one end or the other?"

They continue to stare at me with blank faces, but then they think about it, wondering if maybe I'm on to something. I'm surprised it's the first time they thought about it. The second I entered the creature's guts, it's *all* I could think about. Perhaps they're so used to the job they don't think of it as a living being anymore. They don't think of it as having anatomy. It's just a big, sludgy mountain to them.

"Is it possible?" Sanchez asks Meri.

She pauses, thinking about it. Then she shrugs.

"Nobody's ever done it before," she says. "But I don't see why it won't work."

Hoji jumps in front of Meri, blocking me from her view. "Are you fucking crazy? The maggot doesn't know what the fuck he's talking about. He's never been inside of the intestines. He doesn't know anything."

Meri brushes away his argument. "Yeah, but that doesn't mean he's wrong. It *is* an option. Not a very safe or pleasant one, but a better option than waiting here and praying for rescue."

"There's got to be another way," Bill says.

"I'm open to alternatives?" Meri asks.

They all stare at the floor, trying to come up with something, anything else they can do. But the more they think about it, the more my idea is the only thing that makes sense.

"We'll vote on it," Meri says.

"I say we go," Sanchez says.

"Of course you do," Hoji says. "You got nothing to lose. You're going to die either way."

"Not if I get out of here in time," Sanchez says.

Meri turns to Bill, "What do you think?"

The old guy doesn't make eye contact, shifting his weight to the side, shaking his head. "I don't fucking know. It's too damn crazy." Then he pauses, thinks about for a second. He looks up at Meri. "Fuck it. If you think it's the best option I'll go. I'd rather die trying something."

Hoji is the only one who won't give in.

"Fuck you guys," he says. "I vote no. No fucking way. I'd rather wait here."

Meri shakes her head. "Well, too bad. You've been outvoted.

You're coming with us."

"I'm not doing shit," Hoji says. "The maggot is bad luck. Taking his stupid advice is going to get you all killed."

"You'll do as you're told," Meri says.

Hoji doesn't stand up to her. He sits down in a chair, facing away from us, and gripes to himself. I'm not sure if he'll actually go with us or not, but he doesn't argue any further.

Meri turns to the rest of us. "The big decision now is which direction we should go. Out the throat or out the anus?"

"Anus!" Sanchez says. "They got a Motel 6 there, remember? Remember when I said that?" He laughs at his own joke. "That was some funny shit."

We ignore him. He's probably delirious from the pain.

"Whichever is quickest, I guess," Bill says.

I speak up and ask, "What's the difference?"

Meri says, "Well, if we go down toward the anus, the intestines will get smaller. It might be more cramped. There's also a hell of a lot more of them, so we'd likely have a much farther distance to travel, even though we're closer to the anus than the throat."

"So going through the throat would be better?" I ask.

She shakes her head. "It would be faster, but more dangerous. We'd have to go through the stomach. We *really* don't want to go through the stomach."

"Fuck that," Bill says. "I no longer vote for the quickest route. Let's take the long way. It'll be safer."

"I change my vote too," Sanchez says. "Let's take the stomach if it's quicker."

Meri turns to me. "What do you think? Stomach or small intestines?"

"It doesn't matter," I say.

She says, "You have to vote."

"No," I say, trying to explain. "I mean, it isn't really up

to us, is it? Won't we just take whichever intestine we can get to from the safe room door? We don't really have the time to find the right passageway that will go the direction we want."

Meri nods. "Good point. But if we have both options available, we need to choose. What would be your choice?"

I shrug. "If I had a choice I guess I'd say small intestines."

Sanchez frowns at me. "Ah, come on, Maggot. You really going to outvote me? I'm going to die if we don't get out in time."

"But I'm fine with either one," I say. "You all know more than I do about this place. I don't think I should have a say."

Meri nods. "Well, my vote is small intestines as well. I've seen the stomach before. We don't want to go there if we can avoid it."

"Fine, you bunch of assholes," Sanchez says. "We'll take the safer route."

Meri heads toward the food and water, and starts filling a pack with as much as it can hold.

She looks back at us and says, "Let's get a move on. I want us out of here within the hour."

Once we grab all the food and supplies we can carry, we put on our masks and Meri opens the safe room door.

"Stand back," Meri says, as chunks of meat roll into the room.

There's a wall of meat on the other side. Like an avalanche of flesh had fallen onto the safe room. I have no idea how we're going to get through.

"Pickaxes," she says. "We've got to dig our way to the closest intestine."

Bill and Meri pull out their pickaxes and get to work. With one arm, Sanchez isn't able to help. But at least he is standing now. His legs aren't injured so at least he'll be able to walk. He just can't do anything that requires two arms.

"Get to work," Sanchez tells me, handing me his pickaxe.

It's not exactly a pickaxe. It's bladed on one end, designed to cut through flesh instead of rock.

I look up at the large wounded man, investigating his wound. "Are you going to be okay?"

Sanchez shrugs, trying to duct tape the arm of his rubber suit back together. "Don't worry about me, Maggot. I won't let something this small do me in."

Then he uses his good arm to push me in the direction of the door.

I'm not much use with the pickaxe, but it doesn't take Meri and Bill very long to slice a passageway through the flesh on their own. They cut it apart one slab of flesh at a time, then have me drag the chunk into the safe room with the hook of the axe. The adrenalin gives me a new source of strength. When my survival is on the line, I'm able to actually pull my weight. I'm able to contribute without feeling like a worthless idiot. Bill no longer has any reason to complain about me. Instead, he turns his frustration on Hoji.

"Is he just going to sit there and let us do all the work?" Bill says to me. "Worthless piece of crap. If he's not going to do anything then we should just leave him here to rot."

I just nod at him and haul meat slabs into the safe room, not wanting to join in on the complaining session.

"He's always this way," Bill says. "Always being a little crybaby when he doesn't get things his way. Thinks he's too good for the rest of us."

I don't know why Bill wastes his time complaining about his co-workers. He complained about me all day. Now he's complaining about Hoji. I guess he's the kind of person who always needs something to complain about. It's his way of expressing his frustration, just as anger and throwing tantrums is Hoji's way of expressing it, and making jokes and poking fun at people is Sanchez's way of dealing with it. Everyone has their faults, I guess. I know I have plenty of them. Too many to count.

"Hey Sanchez," Meri calls into the safe room. "Write a note telling them where we went. If we die out here I want them to know what happened to us."

"But if this place collapses how are they going to find it?" he asks.

"They'll find it," she says. "Just do it."

"Sure," Sanchez calls back.

He goes to the white board and writes a note in the worst handwriting I've ever seen. It just says: "Went out the pooper."

Then he laughs at himself.

We only need to dig about twenty feet until we reach the closest intestine. Meri cuts a door into the side of it, revealing a wide open tunnel leading deep into the monster's body.

She peers inside, inspecting the passage.

"This'll have to do," she says.

She steps inside. Bill and I follow. It's much roomier in here than I thought it would be. Like standing in a subway tunnel caked with mud. Only this isn't mud. It's most likely monster feces—half-digested animal and human corpses.

"Watch out for worms," Meri says. "They're probably everywhere."

I look down. The excrement goes halfway up my calves. I don't think I'll be able to see any worms even if they're there.

"Which way are we going?" Bill asks. "Toward the throat or anus?"

"This is a large intestine," Meri says. She points down the passageway, to the left. "So we'll head for the throat."

Bill points in the opposite direction. "But can't we still go this way? Toward the anus?"

She shakes her head. "We've already pulverized and excavated the middle intestines. The passageway won't go very far."

"So we have to…" Bill begins.

"Yeah," Meri says. "We're going to have to go through the stomach."

Bill lets out a sigh and says, "Just great…"

Meri turns to me. "Tell Sanchez and Hoji we're heading out."

I nod and go back the way I came.

Sanchez meets me at the entrance to the safe room.

"How's it going?" he asks. "Any luck?"

I nod. "We got to the large intestine. It's time to go."

"Well, let's go then," Sanchez says.

But when I look at Hoji, the grumpy worker doesn't look like he's planning to go anywhere.

"We're leaving now," I say. "Are you coming with us?"

"Fuck no," he says.

I look back at Sanchez, hoping he'll be of some help. But Sanchez is already gone, leaving me to deal with the disgruntled Samoan.

I step closer to him. "Are you sure you want to stay here? All by yourself?"

"Yeah."

"Even if this place collapses?"

He shrugs. "Just get out of my sight."

The second he says that, the whole building shakes and quivers. The squealing sound of bending metal echoes through the room.

We both look up at the ceiling, praying that it holds. I step slowly back, toward the exit.

"Are you sure?" I ask.

Even though there's fear rattling in his voice, he says, "Yeah. Now leave."

I don't argue with him. I rush toward the exit as another tremor hits the room.

"Well, if your change your mind, you know where to find us," I say.

"I said leave, Maggot," he says.

I add, "Just take a left once you enter the large intestine."

Hoji yells at me, "Not leaving fast enough."

Then I go through the exit and head toward the intestine. When I get back to the others, Bill asks, "Where's Hoji?"

I shake my head. "He refuses to come."

Meri looks at me and says, "Fuck him then. Let's go."

The second she turns around, a loud squealing sound pierces our ears and then there's an eruption. All of us know what it is the second we hear it. It's the safe room collapsing.

"Hoji!" I cry, rushing back to where I left him.

But just outside the intestine, there's nothing but meat. The tunnel we dug out has collapsed back in on itself. The safe room, if it even still exists, is unreachable.

Meri comes up behind me. "He's dead. Forget about him."

The others turn and continue on, but I stay back. Just for a minute. I hear something. A squishing sound. Then a muffled groan. Something's in there.

"Hold up," I tell the others.

A yellow-gloved arm reaches out of the meat. It's Hoji, trying to get through. He must have gotten out of the safe room just before it collapsed, but ended up getting buried in the meat before he could get to us.

"Hoji's still alive," I say.

When Bill and Meri come back, we pull the large man out of the meat avalanche and wipe the slush off of him.

"I thought you weren't coming," Meri tells him, like it's the closest she comes to saying she's happy he's still alive.

"I changed my mind," he says.

She turns away from him, walking through the deep sludge past Sanchez, and tells him, "We've got a long way to go. Don't slow us down."

Then, using only the glowing lights on our suits to guide us, we follow Meri deeper into the bowels of the monster.

PART THREE
OVERTIME

CHAPTER
SEVEN

David and I spent a whole week celebrating the monster's death, as well as celebrating the memories of those we lost. We didn't hate each other like we used to before the attack. We became best friends. We made up for lost time, spending all night just drinking and talking, telling stories about ourselves, learning all sorts of things about each other we never knew before.

We moved into a random house in the Alberta neighborhood, one of the few areas still standing in northeast Portland. The front lawn had a nice view of the monster's corpse. We used to sit outside, drinking warm beers, and just admiring the destruction of the once-indestructible beast. It filled us with joy and hope. It made us think we were capable of anything.

The quarantine they put up around the town didn't bother us too much in the beginning. We couldn't leave town, but at least they gave us rations. We didn't have to worry about getting jobs or paying rent. We were able to just hang out and celebrate life. We were able to be as lazy or idiotic as we wanted.

Since we didn't have electricity or television or the internet, we had to come up with some old-fashioned forms of entertainment. David organized soccer games with the neighborhood children, kicking the ball around in the street with broken fire hydrants as goal posts. David's team relentlessly defeated my team every single time. We also organized a nightly poker game with some of the other adults on the block. We used real money, even though there wasn't much use for it anymore. All stores were closed down so there wasn't anywhere we could spend it.

The neighbors didn't ask us if the house we lived in was our own and we didn't ask them the same question. It was possible that all of us on that block were all squatting in other people's homes, moving in like vultures to take from the dead. But we were happy. We were neighborly. We all had a connection, something that bonded us in a way that neighbors rarely bonded—we all survived incredible odds. We all had a reason to live life to the fullest.

But then came the stench. The giant monster corpse let off its decaying rotting fumes, filling our skies with toxic death. Our happiness turned to misery. We didn't play cards anymore. We didn't play with the neighborhood kids. The only time we spoke to our neighbors was to argue with them. We'd accuse them of stealing our food even though we had no reason to suspect it was them. They'd accuse us of peeping on our wives while they bathed in metal tubs in their backyards even though we had no desire to see them in such a state. Everyone was angry and depressed and searching for people to take out their frustrations on.

There weren't many police officers to manage crime, so looting and violence became increasingly more common. Our food rations were cut in half. Then cut in half again. We were like prisoners cut off from the outside world and there was nothing we could do about it.

My brother and I continued drinking, but it was no longer for the sake of celebration. It was what we did to deal with the pain and depression. I'm not sure where he got the liquor we drank. I'm pretty sure he was stealing it. Maybe even going into the ruins of old neighborhoods and digging them out of cellars that survived the rampage.

But even the booze ran out eventually. The skies became so toxic that we had to wear gas masks everywhere we went. Some days the rot-smog was so bad that we had to sleep with the masks on our faces.

After a month of living in the quarantine zone, my brother and I barely spoke to each other anymore. He went out each day for hours at a time. Then would come back, eat a cold can of soup and go to bed. We spent a lot of our time sleeping. It was the only thing that felt right. It was the only thing that helped us forget about our problems. The monster destroyed our past. The quarantine destroyed our present. And the idea of having any kind of a future at all seemed unlikely. We thought it would just continue like this forever.

One day, I caught David sitting on the couch, injecting something into his arm. At first, I thought it was heroin. But the liquid was bright blue, like cleaning fluid. That was when I thought he was trying to kill himself.

I ran at him and grabbed the syringe out of his arm.

"What the fuck are you doing?" he yelled.

"What the fuck are *you* doing?" I cried. "Are you trying to kill yourself?"

He stood up, reached for the needle, trying to get it back

from me. I hid it behind my back.

"Are you mom now?"

Tears formed in my eyes. I couldn't help it. Back then my emotions ran from dull and apathetic to way too intense. I was having one of those intense days.

"How could you go and commit suicide like that?" I asked. "You're really going to just kill yourself on the couch and leave me all alone? You said no matter what we'd always be together."

When David saw the tears in my eyes, he just laughed at me. It was a forced laugh, with more than a bit of anger in it. The laugh reminded me of the laughs he used back when he bullied me as a child.

"I'm not trying to kill myself, dumbass," he said. "That's an anti-depressant. You think it was Drano or something?"

I looked down at the syringe. It glowed with blue light like it was radioactive. "An anti-depressant? It doesn't look like any anti-depressant I've ever seen."

He took it from my hand. "It's a drug called Blue Food. It's the only thing available on the streets now."

"Is it safe?" I asked. "It's not like heroin is it?"

He shook his head and pulled out a small vial of the fluid. "It's supposed to be safer than alcohol. It's clean. No comedown. No withdrawal. Just a three-hour high that's supposed to be pure euphoria."

"Have you tried it before?" I asked.

"Not yet," he said. "Since there's no weed or alcohol out there anymore, I figured I'd give this a try. I need something, you know? I just can't stand it anymore. Just sitting here being depressed all the time. It's driving me insane."

I nodded at him. "But you don't know what that stuff does. It could make you worse."

He shrugged. "Well, I want to try it out and see. Want

to join me?"

He held out the syringe, but I shook my head. Something about the blue glow didn't seem right. I didn't care if they said it was safer than alcohol. It looks like it's got to be dangerous.

"I'm good," I said, holding out my hands to keep it away.

"Suit yourself." He went back to the couch and sat down.

Although I wouldn't do the drug with him, I decided to stay and watch just in case something went wrong. It wouldn't be easy to get him to a hospital if he overdosed, but I prepared myself for the worst. One guy down the block still had a working vehicle. If anything went wrong I would've had to beg the guy for help. The hospital still had one or two working ambulances, but there were no phones to call them. I just prayed David would be okay.

When he injected the glowing blue fluid into his vein, the drug took immediate effect. David's spine jerked forward, his fingers twitching. My heart skipped a beat. I thought he was going to die right there. But then he let out a long breath and his muscles relaxed. He slid back into the couch cushions and dropped the weight of his head against the wall.

"Oh, man..." he said, as the blue light crawled up his arm, glowing through his skin.

Then he smiled. It was the biggest, stupidest smile I'd ever seen on his face. All his pain and worries slipped away. I could almost feel the happiness radiating off of him.

He opened his mouth and his words came out in what seemed like slow motion. "It's... so... nice..."

Then his eyes changed color. At first, it seemed like I was hallucinating it. The shade in his eyes went in and out, darkening and brightening between his natural color and a glowing icy blue. Then the blue seemed to swirl, like the cornea of each eye had become a miniature whirlpool.

"You've got to try it," he said, trying to hand me the

vial. But he was too weak to lift it more than an inch off the couch. "You've got to... join me in here."

I stepped back. I didn't want any part of that, no matter how good it made him feel.

After his trip was over, he injected himself again. Then he did it again, until the vial was empty.

For days, all David did was take Blue Food. He would go out and get as many vials as he could find and then melt away into the couch. We really didn't speak or hang out anymore, even though he was always around, always getting high.

I would pick up our weekly rations from the food bank and try to get him to eat, but nothing would stay down. He just puked it up onto the carpet or into the sink. Eventually, he stopped bothering.

"I don't need to eat anymore," he said, between trips. "It's called Blue *Food* for a reason. It's full of vitamins and nutrients. I don't need to eat when I'm on it."

"That's bullshit and you know it," I said, trying to push a spoonful of cold tomato soup in his face.

He pushed it away. "It is fine. I'm never hungry on it. Look at me. I'm not withering away. Trust me."

But how could I trust him? He was addicted to the stuff. I had no idea what it was doing to him. But I was convinced it was going to kill him if he kept doing it.

"How do you even pay for that stuff?" I asked. "It's not like we have money or anything to trade."

He shook his head. "They give it away for free."

"What?" I asked. "That's ridiculous."

"You don't know what it's like," he said. "It's so blissful, so magnificent, like being transported to a world of peace on Earth. If I knew how to produce it I would give it away for free as well. This isn't something to profit from. This is something to share. If you could bring happiness to the world wouldn't you want to share it with as many people as possible? That's what this stuff does. It changes your whole outlook on life."

I thought he was full of shit, but at least he was talking to me. It was the most he'd said in weeks.

"You *have* to try it," he told me. "Just try it once. If you don't like it I'll never ask you again."

I shook my head. "No fucking way."

"But you *have* to," he said. Tears formed in his eyes. "It's heaven on earth. I mean that literally. It is exactly what you would think of as heaven. It's perfection."

"I don't care. I don't want to waste my life on that stuff. It's going to kill you."

He shook his head. "No, it's not killing me. It's giving me life." He pointed at the room around us. "*This* is killing *you*. This place. This pathetic excuse for a life. You don't realize it but it is. If you really want to be alive again you'll take it. If you want to be with me again you'll give it a chance."

"No fucking way," I said.

As I walked out of the room, he yelled, "You will. I *know* you will. When you're ready, just ask me and heaven will be yours."

David wasn't himself after that. I didn't recognize him as my brother. Not only did his personality change but so did his body. He seemed to be aging at a rapid pace. His skin wrinkled. His hair started falling out. One morning, I found blood and a tooth in the sink. His muscles became tight and thin. It was like I was living with a complete stranger who slept on my couch and never ate or slept.

Every once in a while, there would be other people in the living room with him. I didn't know who they were or where they came from. They'd sit in a circle on our living room floor, tripping on Blue Food together, their veins glowing with bright radioactive light. But there was something wrong with them. They weren't like heroin addicts getting high together. They seemed to be communicating with each other, speaking to one another using only their minds. It was like they shared the same trip, joining each other in another world, just as David said. Like they were in some kind of blissful heavenly world.

I didn't know how I was going to do it, but I knew I had to get him off the drug somehow. I had to save him as he saved me from the creature all those weeks ago. But I didn't know how.

When I tried stealing his stash, it didn't go well. He reacted violently, like a wild animal. He pushed me against the wall, yelling at me with his toothless mouth wide open. His eyes spinning. Whenever he wasn't on the stuff, his eyes didn't go back to their natural color. Instead they were bleached white, like his cornea had been burned away long ago. It made him look like some kind of ferocious zombie-like creature.

"What the fuck did you do with it?" he asked. "Give it back!"

"I threw it out," I said.

He punched me in the stomach and threw me on the floor. Then he ran out of the house to get more.

It didn't help taking it away from him. Since it was free,

he could get it any time he wanted. What I needed was to figure out a way to detox him. I had to chain him to his bed, get him off of it until he finally came to his senses. But I wasn't sure how safe that was. I was worried he would hurt himself trying to get away. If he really was able to survive on nothing but Blue Food, I wondered how it would affect him to introduce real food to his system.

I went to the hospital and asked them about it. I assumed they would have gotten several of the addicts in there. I was sure they would know much more about it than I did. But when I asked about Blue Food, they had no idea what I was talking about. They said drug overdoses were at an all-time low. No news of a new blue-colored drug had reached them.

I decided I had to just give it a try. I had to try to detox him. Even if it killed him, it would be worth a shot. Because if I did nothing he would surely die on his own. My plan was to wait until he was high on the drug, tripping out in the living room. Then I would chain him to the toilet. When high, he was weak. He wouldn't be able to resist me. Then I would nurse him back to health. When he was sober enough, I would talk some sense into him.

But before I could enact my plan, David was gone. He left home one night and never came back. He didn't say anything. He didn't leave a note. He was just gone.

I spent so many nights wondering what happened to my brother. I assumed he had to have been dead. The drug must have finally killed him or somebody else killed him for it. I'm not sure. Seeing how violent he got when he was off of the drug, I could imagine anything could have happened.

121

A fellow junkie might have turned on him for his stash or maybe somebody killed him in self-defense when he got rabid and angry at them. It's also possible that somebody or something killed him when he was high and too weak to defend himself. There were several packs of dogs roaming the streets, known to attack and kill the many homeless people wandering the city. There were a lot of ways he could've died.

I accepted his death as best I could, but I still missed him. My brother was all I had left. After our mother and father and pretty much everyone else I ever knew had died, it was a comfort knowing I had at least one person left in my life. It made surviving the whole ordeal worth something.

It was difficult getting by without David. But I kept on, just running on auto-pilot. Eating, cleaning, sleeping, trying to keep my mind occupied, that was all there was left to do. I sometimes wondered if I wouldn't have been better off dying with my parents. At least then I wouldn't have had to deal with the deep, unending loneliness that consumed me after that. I just kept telling myself that it would get better. Someday, eventually, it would get better. That was all I had left to hold on to.

CHAPTER
EIGHT

Traveling through the intestine is slow-going. The muck is sometimes waist deep and full of all manner of hazards—large chunks of concrete that trip us up, pieces of jagged metal that can tear through our suits. There are most likely several human bodies resting beneath the sludge, but we try not to think about it.

"Treat this as research, boys," Meri says, leading the way. "Once we get out of here we're going to pulverize this whole place."

Hoji groans. "Once I get out of here I'm quitting. Fuck this job."

"Bullshit, Hoji," Bill tells him. "You always say that."

"This time I mean it."

I walk more carefully than the others, watching my every step, paranoid of what's lurking beneath the sludge. Since I can't see anything under the surface, I watch for movement. If anything is down there I'm sure there would be bubbles or a shift in the fluid. I just have to keep my eyes on the surface at all times.

"What's holding you up, Maggot?" Meri asks me when she sees me lagging behind.

"Worried about tack worms," I say.

"I don't think we have to worry about that," Meri says. She points at the walls. The tunnel is black and charred from the explosion. "When the gas was ignited, it burned through the entire intestinal tract. It probably burned up any tack worms that were living in here."

"Are you sure?" I ask.

"The only worms I've seen so far have been dead," she says.

I nod in relief, but still don't take my eyes off of the sludge.

"Thank God for that," Bill says.

"But there's a downside to the fire coming through here," Meri says. "It killed the worms, but it also burned up most of the oxygen. Have you realized how hard it is to breathe in here? You can thank the explosion for that."

"Are we going to suffocate?" I ask.

"Probably not," she says. "As long as we keep moving."

As we move, I see Sanchez flipping through a stack of photographs. I recognize them as the photos on the memorial board back in the safe room.

"What are you doing with those?" I ask him.

When Sanchez sees me, he pushes the photos back into one stack.

"Nothing," he says. "Just remembering all the people who died down here."

"Were you friends with most of them?"

Sanchez shrugs. "No, I wouldn't call any of the assholes my friends. But I worked with them every day. I spent more time with them than any real friends of mine. I shared memories with them, had a history with them. You know, they were a part of my life. That doesn't make them friends, but it makes them *something*. I still want to honor their memory. I didn't want to leave their pictures behind." He pulls three photos from the stack. "After today, I've got three more to add to the pile." He holds out the photos of Hector, Jake and Mitch. "Hector joined gut crew about the same time as I did. I never thought I'd be adding him to the list. I never thought he'd be one of the losses." Then he puts the photos with the others.

"The day's not over yet, Sanchez," Hoji says, walking behind us, eyeballing the photos over my shoulder. "You'll be adding a lot more than those three to that list before the day's done. Yourself included."

Sanchez puts the photos away. "This beast couldn't kill me when it was alive, Hoji. It sure won't kill me as a corpse."

"We'll see about that."

Up ahead, the tunnel is clogged with the wrecks of vehicles— trucks, hatchbacks, bicycles, even a VW Bus. As we pass them, I can't help but look inside. Most of them are empty, flipped over on their backs, or filled with sludge. But the occupants of the VW Bus still remain. They seem familiar for some reason. People I've met somewhere before. Then I think back to the day the creature fell. The two hippies who offered a ride to David and I. I'm not sure if it's them. It could be. Part of me thinks it has to be.

Two twisted bodies lie still in the front seat. They aren't skeletons like the ones I found while tossing shit earlier in the day. They haven't fully digested yet, perhaps because we're farther up in the intestinal tract than the others were. Their faces are stretched in horror, as though they were alive when the van was swallowed by the creature. I couldn't imagine what that would have been like to be them. I wonder how long they survived in the creature's stomach. Were they digested alive or did they asphyxiate on the gaseous fumes in the creature's stomach? Their hands are tightly clasped together. I wonder if they had enough time to say goodbye to each other before they finally died. I hope they did. I don't know why, but it makes me feel a little better knowing they were able to die together.

"Kimmy?" Bill yells.

I look away from the VW Bus to see the old guy charging past me, racing toward a vehicle up ahead.

"Kimmy!" he screams. "Are you in there?"

He recognizes one of the vehicles, a white Mini Cooper. The thing is bent and crushed and filled with sludge. I'm not sure how he recognizes who this particular vehicle could have belonged to. It's not that uncommon of a vehicle in Portland.

"Stop him," Meri says.

Sanchez tries to get into Bill's way, tries to hold him back. But Bill is delirious. He's eyes are watering in his mask.

"Kimmy's in there," he says. "I know she's in there."

"There ain't no one in there," Sanchez says. "It's just car. You don't know that it's your daughter's car."

"It is her car," he says. "I know it's hers. Look at the stickers on the bumper."

There aren't any stickers on the bumper, but Bill seems to see them. There are rectangular shapes that might have once been stickers, before they were dissolved away. But it's not proof that the vehicle is his daughter's car.

"Let me go," Bill says, pushing on Sanchez. "I have to get her out of there."

Bill accidentally pushes on Sanchez's wounded arm, causing the big guy to scream in pain and loosen his grip. Bill breaks free and runs to the car. He grabs the door handle and tries to open it. But it won't open. It's either locked or jammed shut. He bangs on the window, trying to break through.

"It's not her car," Meri says, charging through the sludge at the old guy.

"It's hers," he cries, trying to wipe away his tears but only rubbing muck on his mask. "It has to be hers. It's one of a kind."

Meri points at the license plate. It's not an Oregon plate.

"It's from California," she says. "Did your daughter have California plates?"

He looks at it and then up at Meri.

"Well, did she?" Meri asks.

Bill lowers his eyes and shakes his head.

"We've all lost people," Meri says. "You're not special."

"I lost my daughter," Bill says, still weeping. "Have you lost a daughter? Do you know what that feels like?"

Meri glares at him. "Of course I know what it feels like. I lost two daughters. And a son. And a husband. And a sister. And both parents. And everyone I ever knew. But I don't lose my shit over a car that might possibly belong to one of them, especially not when the occupants are obviously long dead."

"Yeah, but are you responsible for any of their deaths?" Bill asks. "Did any of them die because you were dead drunk and too messed up to save yourself? Did they risk their lives to come for you even when you didn't give a shit whether you lived or died? Did you tell them to fuck off when they showed up on your doorstep, trying to get you to safety? Did you waste their time by resisting their help, making it so that there was no chance left for them to get away? Did you watch as some giant tentacle ate them up, just after you told them to go to hell and shut the door in their face?"

Bill pauses, his breath heavy and raspy in his suit. He

must have used up most of the oxygen around him.

He points at himself and continues. "Well, that's what I did. And the only reason I work this job and don't shoot myself in the face is because I hope that someday—"

Blood explodes out of Bill's chest as he is attacked from behind. Some kind of reptilian claw tears through his flesh, breaking through his ribcage. Then he is pulled underwater.

"What the fuck was that!" Hoji cries.

Bill gurgles and screams as he's pulled further up the intestine. I don't see what's got him. It moves too quickly.

"Come on!" Meri yells, racing after Bill. She holds up her bladed pickaxe like a weapon.

The rest of us follow her.

Bill's mask is torn off and he chokes and gags on the toxic fumes. Blood oozes from his mouth.

We try to catch up to him, but whatever has him is fast and won't let go. The old guy is pulled far ahead of us, out of sight. We just hear his cries echoing deep into the intestinal cavern. Then there's silence.

"What the fuck was that?" Hoji yells at Meri, as though she's to blame for it.

Meri shakes her head. "Don't look at me. I don't fucking know." She looks down the tunnel. "Some kind of parasite we haven't heard of before."

"What kind of parasite is that?" Hoji says. "That was no fucking tack worm. That was some kind or predator."

"It looked like a lizard man," says Sanchez.

We look at him.

"Lizard man?" Meri asks.

Sanchez nods. "Didn't you see it? It had scales and everything."

"Are you sure?" I ask.

Meri looks at me, then back at Sanchez.

"Yeah, I'm sure," he says. "It looked like the goddamned Creature from the Black Fucking Lagoon."

"That's ridiculous," Meri says.

"That's what it looked like to me," Sanchez says.

"You've lost too much blood," Hoji says. "It's making you go mental."

I don't know what they're talking about. The others saw it, too. Sanchez is just the only one willing to admit it. I didn't see a lizard man, but I did see a claw. It could have been a reptile's claw. We don't know enough about the giant monster to know everything that's lurking inside of him. For all we know, he could have parasites that look like lizard men living inside of him.

Either way, one thing is certain: something dangerous lives inside the creature's intestines. Something that's hunting us. It's going to be even more dangerous getting out of here than any of us realized.

Not knowing what else to do, we continue down the tunnel. But now we don't let down our guard. Hoji, Meri and I all carry pickaxes, ready to strike at anything that comes up from the sludge.

"The stomach should be close," Meri says. "Hopefully the explosion cleared it out. Otherwise, we're fucked."

"Damn right we are," Hoji adds.

Clutching the pickaxe tightly, staring down at the surface

129

of the fluid, I ask, "Why's that?"

"There's too many parasites to get through," she says. "We wouldn't stand a chance unless most of them were killed off."

Sanchez adds, "It's the tack worm breeding ground. There will be thousands of them."

I nod. This new information worries me. I wonder if we made the right decision coming this way. Perhaps we should have tried to go for the small intestines instead, even if it took us longer. But it's too late now. We have to keep pushing forward.

Hoji grows impatient with my slow, cautious steps as he walks behind me. He doesn't seem interested in being careful. He just wants to get out of here as soon as possible.

"Out of my way, Maggot," he says, pushing me aside.

I stumble and fall knee-first into the sludge. The blade of his pickaxe comes an inch away from cutting my ear off as he passes me. Sanchez sees it happen. He looks at me and chuckles.

"What's his problem?" I ask Sanchez as he helps me up.

Sanchez smiles. "Who? Hoji? Take your pick. *Everything's* a problem with him."

I say, "I know he's probably lost some people like the rest of us, but that doesn't mean he should be such a jerk to everyone."

Sanchez shakes his head. "Actually, it's the opposite. Hoji didn't lose anyone."

"Seriously?" I ask.

"His nagging wife, his cranky mother-in-law, his lazy sisters, his five spoiled brats," he says. "They *all* survived. And he's responsible for taking care of all of them. I think that's why he's pissed off all the time. He probably wishes he lost some of them."

"I hated my parents, too. But I wish for anything to have them back."

Sanchez nods. "Yeah, but it's got to be rough raising five

kids in all of this. The stress is probably killing him. You can't blame the guy for taking it out on his coworkers every now and then."

"Easy for you to say," I tell him. "You're twice his size. You'd kick his ass if he messed with you."

"Well, of course." Sanchez laughs. He pounds his chest with his good fist. "Nobody messes with The Sanchez."

When we get to the stomach, our fears are proven true. The place is swarming with parasites.

"Fuck..." Meri says.

The stomach is massive, the size of a football stadium. And the belly is filled with thousands upon thousands of tack worms. It must be hundreds of feet deep. And there's more than just worms. Bigger parasites live here. A giant centipede-looking creature wriggles through the mass of worms. Fat, porcupine-like mollusks slither up the stomach lining. There are also a few reptilian creatures the size of crocodiles with fangs and sharp teeth. Perhaps one of these creatures is what attacked Bill back in the large intestine.

"Looks like the fire got some of them," Meri says, pointing at charred worms near the stomach entrance. "But not enough."

"There's no way we could make it through that," Hoji says.

"No shit," says Sanchez. "They'd tear us apart ten feet in."

"It's okay," Meri says. "We'll go around."

We look at her with questioning faces.

She holds up her pickaxe. "We're going to have to dig around the outside. Eventually we'll get to the esophagus."

"It'll take forever," Hoji says. "That thing is a mile wide."

She says, "Then we better get started."

Then she hacks the blade of the axe down into the intestinal wall.

We chop at the meat for what seems like hours, slicing out a pathway around the stomach. It takes much longer than we hoped. By the time we are all out of breath and hardly able to lift our axes, we still have only gone about twenty feet in. It could take us days to get around it. And we don't have days. Sanchez probably only has hours.

"This is useless," Hoji says. "We're never going to get across."

"Would you rather go through the stomach?" Meri asks.

"I'd rather do something that wasn't so fucking stupid," he says.

"You got a better idea?" she asks.

He glares at her but says nothing

"I thought so," she says.

Then we go back to cutting a path.

Twenty minutes of hacking and we come across something. I lose my balance and swing in the wrong direction, cutting into the meat on our right. The pickaxe goes through with little effort.

"What's with this?" I ask.

They look at me as I chop again. The axe goes through with ease.

"The meat's really soft here," I say. "Tender.

Meri's eyes widen with surprise. "Do it again."

I do as she asks and chop with all my strength. The axe slips out of my hands and falls through, dropping on the other side.

"That's not soft meat," she says. "It's hollow."

Hoji and Meri swing their pickaxes, chopping a large hole into the wall of flesh. There's a wide open area on the other side.

"Help me through," Meri asks.

Hoji and I widen the hole so that she can get to the other side. She hands me back my axe and looks around.

"Holy shit..." she says. "It's a junkie tunnel."

Sanchez freaks out with excitement. "Are you kidding me?"

"God damn!" Hoji cries. "We're saved!"

But I don't share in their excitement. I have no idea what they're talking about.

"What's a junkie tunnel?" I ask.

"Druggies dig them to get at the fire glands," Sanchez says. "They say you can get high as shit if you inject the stuff."

When he says that, something clicks in my brain. "Wait... what does it look like?"

"Fuck if I know," Sanchez says. "I wouldn't touch the stuff. But they call it something like Blue Fire."

"You mean Blue Food?" I ask.

"Yeah, that's the shit. Heard of it before?"

I nod. "My brother was addicted to it. I didn't know it came from the creature."

Sanchez chuckles. "Yeah, not many do. We're not supposed to talk about it outside of work. Don't want anyone else digging around in here trying to get to the stuff."

I couldn't believe it. The drug that took over my brother's life wasn't just some ordinary street drug. It was from the monster this whole time. The god damned creature didn't just kill my mom and dad when it was alive. After it died, it took my brother from me as well.

"But thank god for those crazy fucks," Sanchez says. "This passage will lead us right to the surface. We can get out of here."

"Yeah..." I say nodding my head.

But I'm not ready to celebrate our stroke of good luck. All I can think about is my brother. This fucking creature stole him from me. I can't wait until they tear this whole thing down and burn it away.

"Let's go," Meri says, waving us in.

We crawl through the hole, into the tight passageway. I'm not sure how the junkies dug this place. It looks like they just used axes and shovels. It must have taken them weeks. I wonder how they even figured out how to get to the glands or that the glands would even get them high.

The tunnel goes in two different directions.

"Which way?" Sanchez asks Meri.

She shrugs. Then points at a random path. "Let's try this way. We'll eventually find our way out."

We all agree and follow her through the fleshy tunnel, hunting for the closest exit.

CHAPTER
NINE

The junkie tunnel twists and turns through the monster's corpse, the passageway so thin we can only go one at a time, usually stepping sideways. The tunnels split off in many directions, like a maze of flesh. We take tunnels at random and quickly become lost. It's proving to be a lot more difficult to get out of the corpse than we first thought.

"We're just going in circles," Hoji says.

"No we're not," Meri says.

"Yeah, we are."

Meri groans. "Just shut the fuck up, Hoji."

Meri keeps her eyes on a watch strapped to her wrist every time we come across a junction in the tunnel. There must be a compass attached to it. If we keep going west, we'll eventually get out. At least, that's what I hope.

"Why are there so many tunnels?" I ask.

"Who the fuck knows," Meri says, just as annoyed with me as she was with Hoji. "There's a lot of glands in The Meat. They probably dig in every direction until they find one."

"Why doesn't anyone remove them?" I ask. "If people are digging in here to get to them, wouldn't it be a good idea to cut them out?"

Meri shrugs. "They did at first. But there's a lot of them and the junkies are persistent. Whenever a gland is removed, they just dig new tunnels until they find another one."

"There's also rumors that the glands grow back after they're cut out," Sanchez says.

"How do they do that?" I ask. "I thought the creature doesn't regenerate anymore."

Meri laughs. "The thing regenerates all the time. Why do you think it's taking so long to tear down The Big Meat?"

"I thought it was just really big."

She shakes her head. "No, the thing is constantly regenerating. Most of its flesh is dead. Its organs don't work anymore. But it's still got a little life left in it. The glands are supposed to be the parts that regenerate the fastest. They'll probably be the last thing to go."

I grind my teeth, thinking about my brother's addiction.

"I wish they'd burn them out of here," I say. "They should cut out all the flesh around the glands and burn them away so that they never grow back."

Meri sniffs in her mask. Then she asks, "Why do you give such a shit about it?"

I pause for a moment, wondering if I should tell her. Just talking about what happened to David is upsetting. But I decide to tell her anyway.

"My brother got addicted to the stuff," I say. "I think it killed him."

She nods.

"Yeah, it's supposed to be some pretty nasty stuff," she says. "It fucks with your head. Makes you think you've got psychic powers."

I say, "My brother used to say something like that. He acted like he could read people's minds when he was on it. It really fucked him up."

"I bet," Meri says, nodding her head as she steps through the tunnel. "Who knows what the hell is in that stuff."

We see a light in the passage up ahead. A haunting glowing blue light.

"That's probably one of the glands," Meri says.

"So we went the wrong way?" Hoji asks. "We should be going away from the glands, not toward them."

"Let's just check it out."

The tunnel widens as we approach the blue light. It also becomes brighter, warmer. Like the flesh cavity has its own mini sun.

"There's somebody up there," says Sanchez, pointing ahead of us.

He's right. A man sits, curled up in a ball, leaning against the side of the cavern. He's not moving. He doesn't even seem to be breathing.

"Is he alive?" I ask.

Meri shrugs.

We walk up to him. He looks just like my brother did the last I saw him. His hair and teeth are falling out. His eyes look like tiny blue whirlpools. His veins glow through his skin.

Meri kicks him and he grunts. "Yeah, he's alive. Just barely."

I look at her. "What's he doing in here? Don't they just harvest the stuff and leave?"

Meri shakes her head. "Some of them do. But most of them, once they're completed addicted, stay here so they can be closer to the source."

My eyes widen. "You mean they live in here?"

She nods. "There are hundreds of junkies in The Meat, squatting here like it's an abandoned apartment building. Once they move in, they never go out. I have no idea how they survive without food or water, but I've seen it before.

We had to clear out a whole group of them on the other side of The Meat not too long ago."

I think about it for a minute. I wonder if the same thing happened to my brother. I didn't see him die. He just vanished one day. It's possible that he just crawled into the meat like a drug-addicted parasite to make it easier for him to go on injecting Blue Food without having to get it from dealers.

I ask, "Do you think my brother might be in here? Somewhere?"

Meri shrugs. "It might be possible. But I would forget about him if I were you. Once someone's hooked on the fire gland they're never coming back."

I nod at her, but it's not something I'm willing to accept. If my brother is alive, I have to find him. I have to figure out a way to save him. It's not too late. It *can't* be too late.

Despite everything, despite the deaths and the dangerous situation we've been placed in, it's good news knowing that my brother might still be alive. He could be anywhere inside of The Big Meat, but at least it gives me hope. I can get by on hope.

Walking through the tunnels, we pass more junkies. There are dozens of them, leaning against the walls or lying on the floor, all blissed out in a daze. None of them speak or move. Their breaths are shallow. They hardly look alive. I wonder if they're dying or half-dead.

I look at each one we pass, wondering if David is among them. I'm not sure I would recognize him if he was.

"Why aren't they wearing gas masks?" I ask. "Shouldn't

the toxic fumes infect them?"

Meri shrugs. "I've never seen them wear masks. I don't think they care if it kills them."

But I think she's wrong. I think they are somehow immune to the toxins. Injecting the blue fluid must do something to them, give them a tolerance to the creature's various diseases it emits.

Hoji kicks one of the junkies in the legs. "Hey, asshole. How do we get out of here?"

The junkie doesn't respond. He bends down and looks him in the eyes. Then he snaps his finger in the guy's face.

"You hear me?" he asks. "Where's the exit? We want to get out of here."

But it's no use. The junkie is in his own world. None of them seem to notice we're even here.

"They're not going to help us," Meri tells him. "We're going to have to find our own way out."

The farther down the tunnel we go, the more deformed and warped the junkies become. The ones who have been on Blue Food longer don't have any hair at all. Their eyes look sunken into their heads. Their skin covered in deep wrinkles. Their limbs bony and twisted. They don't look like they can even walk on their shriveled legs. They look totally crippled. I have no idea how they're even able to inject their drugs anymore.

Even farther down, the junkies no longer resemble human beings. They're like creatures. They have scales growing all over their bodies. Claws grow from their fingernails. Spikes grow out of their backs. If they weren't so blissed out I swear they would get up and rip our throats out.

"That's it," Sanchez cries, pointing at one of the junkies. "That's what attacked Bill."

We look at him. His face is dead serious.

"The lizard man," he says. "Bill was killed by one of these junkies."

We look at the drugged out mutants. They don't look like they're capable of attacking anyone. Too comatose. Still, we can't be too careful. Something did kill the old guy. And if it wasn't a parasite it could very well have been one of these mutated addicts.

"Why do they have scales?" I ask, looking up at Meri.

She shakes her head in disbelief. "I have no idea." She leans down for a closer look. "It's like they're transforming into snake people."

"*Lizard* people," Sanchez injects.

"Could the drug really alter their DNA like that?" I ask. "Can it turn them into monsters?"

She has no idea, either. I don't think anyone, not even the government, has seen this before. It's a completely new phenomenon.

"Maybe their skin is just rotting from disease," Meri says. "Maybe it just looks like they have lizard scales."

Sanchez shakes his head. "No way. Look at those claws. They're transforming."

Hoji is standing back from the rest of us, pacing back and forth. This all is freaking him out even more than the rest of us.

"Fuck this shit," he says. "We need to get the fuck out of here. Like *now*."

Meri nods. "I agree. Let's go."

Meri leads us deeper into the tunnel. At the end of the line, the tunnel opens up into a large chamber shining with blue light. In the center is a large blue sphere growing out of the ground. It pulses, wrapped in thick purple veins. It's like a massive eyeball popped out of its socket.

"That's the fire gland?" I ask.

Nobody replies to me, but they don't need to. It's obviously the gland that produces the Blue Food drug.

Surrounding the blue sphere, dozens of reptilian junkies sit around it, staring deep into the glowing light. It's like a god to them. A shrine they worship. None of them move. Just sitting upright like monstrous sculptures.

"There's another tunnel," Meri says, pointing to a cavern opening across the room. "It goes west. That should be the way out."

We creep across the room, stepping over piles of discarded hypodermic needles, moving slowly around the pulsing sphere, keeping our distance from the junkies. Even though they're in blissed out trances, it feels like all their eyes are on us, watching us as we move. When I look back, their eyes are just glowing blue whirlpools. It doesn't look like they're looking at anything, like they don't even have the sense of sight anymore. All they see is the world inside their heads.

I wonder if my brother has become one of these scaled creatures. If he is I'm sure I wouldn't recognize him. I wonder if he'd even recognize me. I wonder if his mind has become as warped as his body. Maybe his memories have dissolved away, removing all recollection of who he was, who his family was. I think Meri might be right. Perhaps it's best if I just forget about my brother. He's probably not savable at this point. But maybe, just maybe, there's still a way.

As Sanchez walks past the glowing blue orb, something inside of his suit lights up.

"What the fuck is that?" Hoji asks him.

Sanchez lifts his arm, his wounded arm. It's filled with blue light, the same light that shines from the orb.

"Something's happening," he says. "It's under my skin."

He unzips his suit and pulls his arm out.

"What the fuck are you doing?" Meri cries. "Put your suit back on."

But Sanchez doesn't listen to her. He lets his rubber suit fall to his ankles and steps out of it.

"The pain is disappearing," says Sanchez.

When he pulls down his sleeve, we see that the glow is coming from his veins. The light glows through his skin in iridescent strips, stretching all the way from his fingers to beyond his shoulders.

"It's the infection," I tell them. "His infected blood reacts to the fire gland."

I'm not sure if I'm right about that, but the others seem to agree.

"It's pulling me closer," Sanchez says, his arm leading him toward the sphere.

"Get away from it," Meri says.

But Sanchez can't help himself. He places his hand on the outer skin of the blue gland. Then he looks back at us.

"I've got to take some," he says.

"What the hell are you talking about?" Meri asks.

Hoji looks around at the creatures around us, gripping his pickaxe tightly. The whole situation is making him more nervous than ever.

"He's gone fucking crazy," Hoji says. "Forget about him. Let's just get out of here."

But Meri refuses to leave Sanchez behind.

"Pull your hand away and step back," she says in the calmest tone she can muster.

Sanchez doesn't move.

"If I don't take it I'm dead," he says.

"What do you mean?" Meri asks.

"Look." He points at the glowing veins in his arm. The blue light stretches past his collarbone and into his chest and neck. If it is the infected areas that are glowing, it means the infection has already spread too far to save him. He's going to die. "I'm all out of options, Chief. I think it's the only thing that will save me."

"Are you fucking kidding me?" Meri asks. "Do you want to turn into one of these mindless freaks?"

Sanchez looks down at them, then shrugs. "It's better than dying."

Before we could stop him, he bites into his arm and reopens the wound. As blood geysers out of the artery, he stabs his arm through the skin of the gland and buries it all the way up to his wound. He doesn't need a syringe to take the drug. The blue fluid enters his artery on its own, pulling itself into his bloodstream. The glowing light spreads across his body, illuminating his skin.

An electrical volt attacks his system, then his muscles relax. His eyes begin to swirl. When he pulls his arm out, his wound has been healed. There is no sign it had ever been cut.

"Holy shit..." Hoji says.

Meri and I are thinking the same thing. Sanchez was right. He did need to take the drug in order to survive. The three-hundred-pound man takes four steps away from the gland and lowers himself to the fleshy ground. He removes his mask, curls up into a ball, and lets a smile widen across his face. He doesn't respond to us when we ask him if he's okay.

"What are we going to do?" I ask. "We can't carry him."

"We're going to have to leave him," Meri says, moving away from her drugged out crewman. "Maybe we'll have somebody come back for him after we get out of here."

Hoji nods. He's just fine with that plan. But when I look down at the large guy, the one who was always laughing and cheering the rest of the crew up, even if it was at my expense, I can't help but wish we could do more for him. I wonder if I shouldn't take the photos out of his pocket, the photos he kept safe to remember his lost coworkers. But I decide to leave them with Sanchez. Perhaps they'll help him to remember who he was, keep him human long enough for us to put a rescue party together and come back for him later.

But as we leave the chamber, I can't help but think that's never going to happen. When we get out, *if* we get out, nobody's going to come back in here just to save a lowly gut crew worker blissed out on drugs.

When we leave the gland chamber, my skin curls. My stomach becomes queasy. I feel like I'm hungover or having a chemical withdrawal. Everything in my body wants me to go back to the fire gland and bask in the light of the blue sphere. Judging by the looks on Hoji and Meri's faces, I can tell they're feeling the same way. We didn't even inject the drug, but were still affected by it in some way. It's like we got some small contact high just from seeing it. Its light rays are enough to enter our bodies through our eyes.

But we fight the urge to go back. It's not too late for us. We can still get out.

"We still have a long way to go," Meri says, staring at her compass. "If we keep moving we should get out by the morning."

"Isn't it morning out there already?" Hoji asks. "It's got to be ten or eleven by now."

"I mean tomorrow morning," she says.

Hoji shakes his head. He can't even begin to express his disappointment in those words.

As we walk down the wet shaft, moving away from the blue light, I see movement in the corners of my eyes. At first, I think it's just the walls pulsing around me, crawling with tack worms. But when we pass an intersection in the passage and I swear I see a human-shaped figure crawling on all fours across the ground. It moves so quickly that it's gone by the time I look in its direction.

"I don't think we're alone in here," I tell the others.

They ignore me. I don't think they want to believe me, don't want to let paranoia get a hold of them.

But then they see it too. Another figure crawls across the ceiling up above us—a reptilian creature similar to the junkies back in the cave. Only these aren't in a dormant trance.

"Just keep going," Meri says, her voice in a whisper. "Try to stay quiet."

We continue hiking through the tunnels. More of the figures show themselves. They claw through the meat, creating new tunnels in the flesh. They are behind us, in front of us, racing through every side-tunnel we pass. They've got us surrounded.

"This is fucked," Hoji says, gripping his pickaxe, ready to swing at anything that gets in range. "We shouldn't be here. We need to go back."

"We're not going back," Meri says.

I turn around and see at least three of the freaks behind us, walking on all fours, stalking us.

"We *can't* go back," I say.

We push on, waiting for the creatures to attack us. But they never do. They just follow us, tracking our movements. After a few hours of hiking through the tunnels, we can't go on any farther. We haven't slept in over a day. We need to rest.

"We'll stop here for a while," Meri says, once we find a wide alcove in the tunnel.

"What about those things?" Hoji asks.

Although he complains, that doesn't stop him from dropping to the ground and getting off of his feet. I'm even more exhausted than he is. I can't even bend my knees to sit down. I just have to drop to the ground, collapse against the wet rotten flesh.

"We're going to have to keep watch," Meri says.

We get as comfortable as we can in our rubber suits, leaning against the squishy walls. We hold our pickaxes in one hand, just in case, and drink water packets in the other—the straws poking under the gas mask, holding our breaths with each sip we take. When the odor gets inside my mask, I choke and wheeze, trying not to puke up the water. It's even more difficult to eat. The food mush combines with the stench to form a rancid meat flavor in my mouth. I can only get down a few bites before I give up, tossing the mostly-full food pouch on the floor.

Only Meri is able to get any sleep. Hoji and I can't sit still, can't relax enough to lose consciousness. Getting off of our feet for a while helps, but it isn't going to rejuvenate us very much. In fact, I have no idea how I'm even going to get back up again. There isn't any sign of the creatures nearby. That's a relief. But I'm sure they're nearby, somewhere. Their lack of presence doesn't help me sleep any better.

Even though we're awake together, Hoji and I don't say

a single word to one another. He really doesn't like me. I don't think he really likes anybody. But I hope we both pull through this together. Even though he's an asshole, even though he' doesn't care if I live or die, I still want him to survive. I want to be able to see him on the other side, maybe even have a drink with him someday. I'm sure he's not really as bad of a guy as he seems.

When Meri wakes up, she doesn't care that we haven't even fallen asleep yet. She gets to her feet, gets her things together, and tells us to move out.

"Get the fuck up or I'm leaving you both," she says, walking forward through the tunnel.

Now that I think about it, Meri's just as big of an asshole as Hoji sometimes. I can't believe I'm stuck here with the two of them.

One of the creatures is in our path, blocking our way through. We stop in our tracks, watching it, keeping our distance.

"What's it doing?" Hoji asks.

"No idea," Meri answers.

The thing doesn't seem to be doing anything at all. It's just lying there. Its limbs folded beneath its chest. We move closer, one step at a time, but it doesn't react. Holding our axes up, ready to swing, we walk right up to it. The thing still doesn't move.

"Is it dead?" I ask.

Meri kicks it and the thing flops to one side. "I think so..."

But when Meri steps on it, her boot sinks all the way through the creature, flattening it to the floor. It's like she's stepping on a pile of old clothes.

"It's not one of them..." she says. "It's just its skin."

"Are they shedding?" I ask. "Like real reptiles?"

She nods, lifting the man-shaped coat of skin with the hook of her pickaxe.

"They're getting bigger," she says, then tosses the husk on the floor.

As we continue farther down the tunnel, we find more of the reptile skin. We examine each one, trying to see if Meri's theory is correct. But none of them are larger than human-sized. If they aren't shedding their skin because they're growing larger, as reptiles do, then why are they shedding at all? Also, the hides are thick and gooey inside. They don't look like they were removed in a normal molting process. It's more like they were hollowed out, like their insides melted away, leaving only the skin. I wonder if this is what the drugs do to people. I wonder if it eventually dissolves them from the inside out.

A blue light shines from the tunnel ahead.

"Another gland?" I ask.

Meri nods. "Looks like it."

But when we see where the light is coming from, it is not another blue sphere. The cavity is several times larger than the last one. In the center, there is a massive lake of blue fluid. It's similar to the fluid from the fire glands, but this is thicker and more viscous. It gently swirls and bubbles. A smoldering heat emanates from beneath the surface, warming the vast chamber. It's like a pit of blue lava.

"What the hell is that?" Hoji asks.

Meri slowly shrugs at him, unable to take her eyes off the swirling liquid. "It's like they collected fluid from all the glands and made a swimming pool with it."

Hoji shakes his head. "Not that." Then he points at something else, by the edge of the pool. "*That.*"

It's one of the lizard men. He stands by the water's edge, writhing and pulsing. It looks bloated. Fatter than the other lizard men. Like a swollen water balloon.

When Meri sees it, she squints her eyes and says, "What's it doing?"

The creature slices open its abdomen, using its own claws to cut through its scales. Like a winter coat, the thing unzips its flesh and lets it slide to the ground. A blue light shines from the insides of the husk and a new figure steps out of it. The thing is man-shaped, but without any features. No eyes or nose or mouth or hair. No genitals or fingernails. It is a being of pure ooze, made up of nothing but the glowing blue liquid. Its flesh drips and swirls as it steps out of its skin and creeps toward the lake.

When we look around, we realize there are dozens of the hollow skins all around us. All of these creatures have torn away their physical forms and entered the swirling pool. Meri was wrong about the shedding reptiles. They weren't becoming larger. They were becoming something else entirely.

"It's joining the others," I tell them.

The man-shaped slime enters the pool of glowing waters and begins to melt. His flesh loosens and flows apart. Then he is gone, completely dissolved into the swirling liquid, becoming a part of it. The lake isn't just a collection of fire gland fluid. It is a massive collection of dozens, maybe hundreds, of those who were once human beings. They have joined together into one conglomeration, forever unified.

I walk up to the shore of the radiant lake and stare into

the ooze. I wonder if my brother is in there, already joined with the others. If that's the case then I really am too late. There really is no way I can save him. How can you separate his liquid from the others?

As I reach out to touch the fluid, my ears are attacked by a series of high-pitched cries. I stagger back and look around. We are surrounded by dozens of the reptilian creatures. They scream at us, snarling and gnashing their teeth, squatting on all fours like tigers ready to attack.

"Let's get out of here," Meri says.

We don't argue with her. When she runs for the nearest exit, we follow.

We take a new tunnel, hoping it doesn't lead to a dead end. The creatures come after us. I'm not sure why they're attacking now when they didn't before. Were they waiting to build up their numbers or was it because we invaded their inner sanctum? Whatever the case, they mean to rip us apart, just as they did to Bill.

"They're too fast," Hoji says, "We'll never outrun them."

"Just keep going," Meri says.

Hoji says, "We have to stand and fight."

Meri shakes her head. "We wouldn't stand a chance."

But Hoji doesn't listen to her. He halts his retreat and raises his pickaxe, ready to hold his ground. Meri and I keep running.

"Don't be an idiot," Meri cries. "Keep going."

Hoji doesn't obey. He's made up his mind and there's nothing she can say to change the stubborn bastard's mind.

"Help me you, you bitch," Hoji yells, as the creatures

close in on him.

But Meri isn't an idiot. She knows we have no hope of killing that whole horde of freaks. I look back and see Hoji swing his pickaxe. He hits two of them with the blade of his weapon, but it isn't strong enough to pierce their thick hides. They tear through his chest and arms with their razor-sharp claws. Then they lunge at him, throw him to the ground and pile on top of him like a pack of rabid wolves.

His screams echo through the tunnel as they rip him to shreds, but we don't go back for him. Meri doesn't even flinch at his death, like it serves him right for not listening to her.

Hoji didn't succeed in killing a single one of them, but his death wasn't for nothing. His death bought us time to escape. Even though he was a selfish asshole who only cared about himself, he ended up sacrificing his life to save ours. He inadvertently did something selfless and heroic. Perhaps, deep down, he even knew what he was doing. Perhaps, deep down, he was a good guy after all.

The adrenalin rush doesn't keep us going for long. Our bodies are weak and malnourished. We can't run as fast as the rabid creatures. Lagging behind Meri, I'm sure that I'll have to be the next sacrifice. Like Hoji, my death will have to help Meri get away. I'm just not fast enough to keep up.

A blue light brightens the tunnel ahead of us. We keep going until we make it into the next chamber. The fire gland pulses and shivers in our direction.

"Is this the same one?" I ask Meri the second we arrive, catching my breath. "Did we go back to where we started?"

We look around the room. It doesn't look familiar. Sanchez isn't lying on the floor where we left him. It must be a different gland than the last one.

The room is full of scaled men just like the last one, but these do not ignore us as we invade their territory. They snap out of their trances, pull themselves to their feet. Meri and I find ourselves completely surrounded.

"There's too many of them," Meri says, pointing her axe blade at the approaching freaks.

I turn around and look into the warm, glowing blue light. There's only one option I can think of. I don't know if it will work, I don't know if it's worse than letting the creatures rip us to shreds, but it's the only idea I have left.

"We have to take it," I say to her.

She looks at me. I point at the blue sphere.

"What?" she asks. "Are you fucking insane?"

I try to convince her. "If we take the drug we'll become one of them. They won't attack us if they think we're one of them."

Meri shakes her head. "But then we'll be fucked. Do you really want to become addicted to that stuff? Do you want to be one of those brain dead junkies, and then one of those mutant creatures? Do you really want to melt into a puddle of blue goo?"

She swings her axe at one of them that gets too close. She doesn't connect with it, missing by inches. The thing dodges her strikes, but doesn't strike back. Not yet, anyway.

"That won't happen unless we keep taking it," I say. "Maybe we'll be fine with just one dose. Maybe we'll have enough willpower to still get out of here before we become like them."

Meri looks at me, then back at the creatures. She doesn't seem able to make up her mind.

"It's a better chance than fighting our way out of here," I tell her.

I bend down and search the floor, looking for syringes. There are several of them. Many of them broken, shattered. But I find two that can still work. I stick the needles, one at a time, into the glowing blue sphere. It pulses and writhes against my knuckles, soothing me with its fleshy warmth. When both needles are full of the blue drug, I hold one out to Meri.

She looks at it like I'm holding a venomous snake, but she still takes it.

The creatures close in, ready to tear our throats out. But the second Meri lowers her pickaxe, the second we hold the needles up to our arms, the creatures hold their position. It's like they're waiting to see what we do next, waiting to see if we go through with it.

"You better be right about this," Meri tells me.

She pulls her arm out of her rubber suit and rolls up her sleeve.

"Just be strong," I tell her. "No matter how good it is, no matter how much you love it. Don't take the drug a second time."

Meri nods.

"I can do it," she says, piercing the needle into her arm. "I've never been addicted to anything in my entire life."

When she injects herself, she collapses right to the floor. At first, I think it's killed her. I worry she might have had an adverse effect to the drug. But then I see her breathing. I see the smile curl on her lips.

I go next. With the creatures staring at me with their swirling whirlpool eyes, I remove my clothing. I scan my arm for a vein. My fingers shake. I've never injected anything before. I worry I might mess it up. But I don't have time to fuck around. The creatures seem to be growing impatient. I make my best guess, stabbing it into what looks like a vein. When I draw a bit of blood into the syringe, I assume I've got it.

The second I push the fluid into my body, a burst of cold electricity crawls through my flesh. It feels like all the molecules that make me one solid being are violently pulled apart. But then the warmth floods in. My skin goes loose, malleable, and every part of me that is ugly—my hate, my fear, my sadness, my loneliness—is washed away. In its place, happiness and comfort blossoms. It takes me over. I see now what my brother was talking about when he described the drug to me. It is pure beauty. It is like heaven is taking over my body.

I let myself slip to the ground, cuddling myself into the rotten, rancid meat. But it no longer disgusts me. The flesh is soothing. Even the foul stench is like fresh flowers to my senses.

And when the drug fully takes over my mind, I can feel my eyes spinning inside the sockets. I can feel another world opening up, one that had always been there the whole time, waiting for me to find its door and walk right in. The only way I can describe the feeling is like coming home after a long, horrible journey.

CHAPTER
TEN

I'm sitting on my couch, doing homework and watching old cartoons. Mom is in the kitchen, baking cookies. Dad is in his office, laughing at stupid Internet memes his brother sent him on Facebook.

The cookie smell fills the living room. I've never been incredibly fond of the taste of cookies, or any desserts for that matter, but there's never been anything more comforting than the smell of baking cookies on a cold winter Sunday.

I get up and go into the kitchen to be with my mother. I don't know why, but I just feel like I have to give her a big hug. It feels like I haven't given her a hug in a very long time and it's just something I need right now.

When I enter, she isn't there. I swear I heard her in here only moments ago, but now she's nowhere in sight. But when I turn around to leave, I feel her wrap her arms around me. I don't see her arms. I don't feel the weight of her flesh. But, somehow, her presence is still here, still hugging me like a warm cloud of emotion. No matter where I step in the kitchen, the feeling of being held by her follows me. It's like the entire room, all the air and furniture and dishes are a part of her. Even the cookies baking in the oven are like her kisses against my cheek.

When I go into my dad's office, it's the same thing. He isn't there. Only the feeling of him exists. His ghost. I can smell his cologne in the room. I can hear his laughter. I can even sense the weight of his ass on his overstuffed leather office chair. But the room is empty.

"I was wondering when you'd come," David says when I return to the living room.

He enters through the front door. I can't see the neighborhood through the doorway behind him. It's like the neighborhood doesn't exist—just a swirl of colors and emotions that don't seem to connect to anything tangible.

"David?" I ask. "Where have you been?"

He closes the front door and motions for me to sit on the couch. I follow him. I'm not sure why I asked him where he's been. I don't remember him ever being gone. But for some reason I get the sense that I've been looking for him, like I thought I'd never see him again. It seems ridiculous. David has always been here, just as I always have.

"I knew you'd come, eventually," David says. "I'm happy you finally made it."

"What are you talking about?" I ask him.

"You've joined the glow," he says. "You're not really back home. This is just a world you created in your head. It is the place that you most yearned for, the place that was so important to you that your subconscious mind solidified it into being."

When David says this, my memories return. I can feel the soft flesh of the meat ground I'm lying on, the smell of the rotting meat. I feel like I'm in two worlds at once.

"So this is just the drug?" I ask him. "None of this is real?"

"It's real, but not in the way you're meaning. It's not a part of the tangible world."

"I don't understand." I shake my head. "David, where have you been? I thought you were dead."

"I'm sorry I left you like that, but I knew I'd see you again eventually. I knew you'd come to the glow, where you belong."

"Are you one of those freakish creatures out there?" I ask, pointing outside the window, even though I mean outside my mind. "They killed two of my friends."

He shakes his head. "I'm no longer in touch with my physical body. I gave it up long ago."

I wonder if that means he's entered the lake of blue fluid, dissolved into the great mass.

"It might be hard for you to believe, but I've been in the glow for many, many years. It might have just been weeks, maybe months, to you. But to me it's been lifetimes. I'm no longer the same person you remember from the old world."

I nod, even though I'm not sure exactly what he's talking about. He does seem different. Even though he looks the same as he did before he started taking the drug, even before the monster attacked and destroyed our home, he still seems to be a completely different person.

"I have so much to show you," he says. "The glow is thousands and thousands of worlds combined into one. Every person that joins us expands our universe. We share each other's thoughts and experiences. We live each other's lives. It's not just pleasant memories like this one. We also create new worlds, new utopias, out of our dreams and fantasies. We are like gods here, living in a paradise of infinite possibilities."

I shake my head. "But none of it's real. Even if you live in a paradise in your minds, your bodies are back in that monster's rotting corpse, just lying there, mutating in a comatose state. How can you accept that?"

David nods. "I understand you might feel that way. It's a scary thought to sacrifice your physical form. But once you've been in the glow long enough, you won't care. It becomes meaningless. There's nothing in your old life that can possibly be as beautiful or fulfilling as your time spent in the glow."

He stands up from the couch and holds out his hand.

"Come with me," he says. "I'll show you."

I don't care what he has to show me. I don't want this. I don't want to give up my life for this place, no matter how much of a paradise it is.

But despite my words, I still get up from the couch and take my brother's hand. Even if I refuse his world, refuse to join what he calls the glow, I'm still not ready to say goodbye to my brother. I still don't want to let him go.

David takes me to worlds beyond my imagination. He shows me fields of elephant-sized strawberries, forests filled with massive flying jellyfish, and cities of mushroom people who speak a strange language using only spores that I somehow completely understand. He introduces me to his friends, people he's known for lifetimes in the glow. Together, we create a new universe, one made of cloud-like roads and buildings of crystal. I meet a woman more beautiful than anyone I've ever seen with shining yellow skin and rainbow hair. I'm not sure if she's someone from the real world or someone I created in my head, but we fall in love and have a romantic affair that seems to last for years.

By the time it's over and the drug begins to wear off, I wish I would never go back. I wish I could stay there in the glow, with my brother, with the dreamlike rainbow-haired woman. I want to experience more of these great wonders.

Just as David said, the real world seems meaningless in comparison. How could I ever go back?

But when the visions fade, I am jerked back into reality. My eyes clear, return to normal. Hovering above me, I see Meri. She smacks me in the face until I'm fully conscious. Then she pulls me to my feet.

"Come on," she says. "We have to get out of here."

I shake the worlds from my head, trying to balance myself, get a grip on reality.

"How long was I out?" I ask.

"Hours," she says.

I take a deep breath, pull my suit back over my body. "It felt like years."

"We can go now," she says. Then she points at the creatures on the ground. "They won't attack us anymore."

I nod and allow her to pull me with her, toward the tunnel. But the glowing blue sphere calls to me, tempting me to come back to the glow. I want to go there again. I don't want to leave.

I tear myself out of her grip.

"No," I say, moving back to the sphere. "I need more. I need to go back there."

She grabs my arm and holds my wrist tightly.

"You have to resist," she says. "Don't you remember? You said we had to be strong. We can't take a second dose."

I shake my head. "I don't care what I said. The glow is so much better than real life. Didn't you experience it? Didn't you see what I saw?"

Meri looks back at the glowing sphere. She knows exactly what I'm talking about. Even though she's strong, I can tell she's tempted to return just as much as I am.

She shakes her head at the thought. "It's not real. I don't give a shit about that place. I want to get out of here."

"You really want to go back to your old life?" I ask her.

"You'd rather live in this toxic city. Work your shitty job. Don't you want something better?"

But my words don't seem to persuade her.

"You don't understand," she says. "This is bigger than you think. We have to get out and warn everyone. We have to put a stop to this."

I have no idea what she's talking about. "Why?"

She explains, "After I woke up, I couldn't pull you out of your stupor. So I left you. I explored the tunnels, looking for a way out. Because the creatures no longer attacked, I investigated that pool of blue fluid. Do you know what it really is?"

She looks me in the eyes. I shake my head.

"It's embryonic fluid," she says. "The bodies of these junkies are being used to create a new creature. A baby."

"That's impossible."

"Well, it's true," she says. "I've seen it with my own eyes. I think all of this is part of the creature's life cycle. The glands, the drug, the junkies... I think it is designed to create offspring after the creature dies." Then she points back at the blue sphere. "If you take any more of that drug then you will help create another monster. You will be contributing to the end of the human race. Is that what you want?"

I look at the blue glow. A part of me doesn't care about the consequences. It wants to go back to David, back to that dream world. But another part of me knows that it's a horrible thing to do. If I allow another monster to be born then all those people died for nothing. My mom, my dad. They wouldn't want me to throw my life away as David did, no matter how magnificent it felt to be inside of the glow.

"Fine, let's go," I say. "Get me out of here before I change my mind."

Meri doesn't hesitate. She grabs me by the arm and pulls me as far as she can away from the blue light.

Once we are in the dark, in the cold rotting meat tunnels, I find it harder and harder to continue. All I want to do is go back. I want to fill my veins with pure euphoria, return to the paradise my brother showed me. But Meri keeps me going. She walks behind me, shoving me every step of the way. I know I wouldn't be able to do it on my own. If it wasn't for Meri I would have gone right back the first chance I got, no matter the consequence, no matter what it did to the rest of the world.

If only Meri wasn't here it would all be fine. I could go back. It's all her fault that I'm not in the glow at that very moment. Why did she have to tell me about the new monster growing in the fluid? Why did she have to let me know about the consequences of taking the blue? If I didn't know about all of that it would have been so much easier. I wouldn't be guilted into going back to my horrible, miserable life. I wonder if she's wrong. It's possible that her theory about the blue lake creating a new monster is just that: a theory. There's no proof. How could she know for sure? She's just doing this on purpose. She just doesn't want me to go back. She doesn't want me to be happy. Hoji was right about her the whole time. She's just a fucking bitch.

I realize that's the answer. That's what I've got to do. Hoji's body should still be in the tunnel up ahead. His pickaxe will surely still be with him. If I can just get it, without Meri knowing. When she's not looking… Meri wouldn't expect it from me. She wouldn't see it coming.

I don't like the idea of killing another human being, but it'll be better if she is dead. It'll be so much easier. Sure, I'll be guilty if I do it. Sure, I'll feel like a horrible, evil person. But once I inject the blue light, my guilt will fade away. The evil in me will disappear. It will be like it never happened.

"Keep going," Meri says, shoving me in the back.

I turn to her and nod my head.

"You bet I will," I say. A smile creeps across my face. "I'll keep going."

I pick up my pace. "That's all I have to do. Keep going..."

Up ahead, I see the shredded remains of Hoji's body. The glint of the pickaxe sends a spin through my eyes.

"I'm just about there..."

BONUS SECTION

This is the part of the book where we would have published an afterword by the author but he insisted on drawing a comic strip instead for reasons we don't quite understand.

I hope you liked my new book, *The Big Meat*. Wasn't it squirmy?

Like many of my recent books, I wrote *The Big Meat* on the Oregon Coast.

I usually work on the back porch where I can smoke cigarettes, drink beer, and enjoy the ocean air.

Unfortunately, this trip was a little different than normal because I went in the middle of October during the rainy season, so it was very cold, wet, and windy outside.

But I didn't let that stop me. I consider myself a very determined person. Once I start a book, I won't let anything get in my way until it's finished.

I refused to let bad weather get in the way of finishing *The Big Meat*, either. I went to the store and bought some umbrellas and rigged them up all over the place, using duct tape, broom handles, and other household items.

Even though there was a pool of water under my laptop and seat and I seemed dangerously close to being electrocuted several times while the laptop was plugged in, it managed to work out for me.

But the gusts of wind that blew over my whole set up once an hour were kind of annoying.

Not to mention all the spiders building webs beneath the umbrella and landing in my face while I was working.

It also wasn't too fun when the water started damaging my laptop one key at a time.

First, the question mark stopped working and I had to copy and paste question marks from other documents.

Then the letter B died.

Then the letter E.

Then half the numbers.

Then the backspace.

By the time I lost the space bar, I realized I wouldn't be able to continue and had to buy a new laptop.

CHEAPO FRED MEYER LAPTOP

There was this raccoon that kept visiting me from time to time, wondering what I was doing. It seemed to be attracted to my cigarette smoke whenever I lit up, probably thinking I was barbequing out there or something.

Vince Kramer, who came with me to work on his book *Hell of Death*, thought the raccoon was cute and fed it a bunch of chocolate pop tarts.

The next day, the raccoon came back with a shitload more raccoons.

I was surrounded by them and they wouldn't leave. They hissed and growled when I tried to scare them away.

They crawled under my table and chair, clawing at me until I gave them more pop tarts.

When we ran out of pop tarts, I had a raccoon riot on my hands.

But I was not going to let them get in my way. I still had a book to write.

I still murdered them all, though.

Not because they messed up my book or anything.
I was just really freaked out that there were
raccoons that knew how to read and write.

Don't tell me you wouldn't do the same thing.

That shit was fucked up.

THE
END

ABOUT THE AUTHOR

Carlton Mellick III is one of the leading authors of the bizarro fiction subgenre. Since 2001, his books have drawn an international cult following, despite the fact that they have been shunned by most libraries and chain bookstores.

He won the Wonderland Book Award for his novel, *Warrior Wolf Women of the Wasteland*, in 2009. His short fiction has appeared in *Vice Magazine, The Year's Best Fantasy and Horror #16, The Magazine of Bizarro Fiction,* and *Zombies: Encounters with the Hungry Dead,* among others. He is also a graduate of Clarion West, where he studied under the likes of Chuck Palahniuk, Connie Willis, and Cory Doctorow.

He lives in Portland, OR, the bizarro fiction mecca.

Visit him online at **www.carltonmellick.com**

QUICKSAND HOUSE

Tick and Polly have never met their parents before. They live in the same house with them, they dream about them every night, they share the same flesh and blood, yet for some reason their parents have never found the time to visit them even once since they were born. Living in a dark corner of their parents' vast crumbling mansion, the children long for the day when they will finally be held in their mother's loving arms for the first time... But that day seems to never come. They worry their parents have long since forgotten about them.

When the machines that provide them with food and water stop functioning, the children are forced to venture out of the nursery to find their parents on their own. But the rest of the house is much larger and stranger than they ever could have imagined. The maze-like hallways are dark and seem to go on forever, deranged creatures lurk in every shadow, and the bodies of long-dead children litter the abandoned storerooms. Every minute out of the nursery is a constant battle for survival. And the deeper into the house they go, the more they must unravel the mysteries surrounding their past and the world they've grown up in, if they ever hope to meet the parents they've always longed to see.

Like a survival horror rendition of *Flowers in the Attic*, Carlton Mellick III's *Quicksand House* is his most gripping and sincere work to date.

HUNGRY BUG

In a world where magic exists, spell-casting has become a serious addiction. It ruins lives, tears families apart, and eats away at the fabric of society. Those who cast too much are taken from our world, never to be heard from again. They are sent to a realm known as Hell's Bottom—a sorcerer ghetto where everyday life is a harsh struggle for survival. Porcelain dolls crawl through the alleys like rats, arcane scientists abduct people from the streets to use in their ungodly experiments, and everyone lives in fear of the aristocratic race of spider people who prey on citizens like vampires.

Told in a series of interconnected stories reminiscent of Frank Miller's *Sin City* and David Lapham's *Stray Bullets*, Carlton Mellick III's *Hungry Bug* is an urban fairy tale that focuses on the real life problems that arise within a fantastic world of magic.

BIO MELT

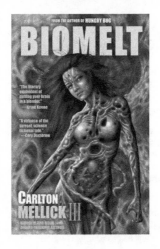

Nobody goes into the Wire District anymore. The place is an industrial wasteland of poisonous gas clouds and lakes of toxic sludge. The machines are still running, the drone-operated factories are still spewing biochemical fumes over the city, but the place has lain abandoned for decades.

When the area becomes flooded by a mysterious black ooze, six strangers find themselves trapped in the Wire District with no chance of escape or rescue. Banding together, they must find a way through the sea of bio-waste before the deadly atmosphere wipes them out. But there are dark things growing within the toxic slime around them, grotesque mutant creatures that have long been forgotten by the rest of civilization. They are known only as clusters--colossal monstrosities made from the fused-together body parts of a thousand discarded clones. They are lost, frightened, and very, very hungry.

THE TERRIBLE THING THAT HAPPENS

There is a grocery store. The last grocery store in the world. It stands alone in the middle of a vast wasteland that was once our world. The open sign is still illuminated, brightening the black landscape. It can be seen from miles away, even through the poisonous red ash. Every night at the exact same time, the store comes alive. It becomes exactly as it was before the world ended. Its shelves are replenished with fresh food and water. Ghostly shoppers walk the aisles. The scent of freshly baked breads can be smelled from the rust-caked parking lot. For generations, a small community of survivors, hideously mutated from the toxic atmosphere, have survived by collecting goods from the store. But it is not an easy task. Decades ago, before the world was destroyed, there was a terrible thing that happened in this place. A group of armed men in brown paper masks descended on the shopping center, massacring everyone in sight. This horrible event reoccurs every night, in the exact same manner. And the only way the wastelanders can gather enough food for their survival is to traverse the killing spree, memorize the patterns, and pray they can escape the bloodbath in tact.

THE BIG MEAT

In the center of the city once known as Portland, Oregon, there lies a mountain of flesh. Hundreds of thousands of tons of rotting flesh. It has filled the city with disease and dead-lizard stench, contaminated the water supply with its greasy putrid fluids, clogged the air with toxic gasses so thick that you can't leave your house without the aid of a gas mask. And no one really knows quite what to do about it. A thousand-man demolition crew has been trying to clear it out one piece at a time, but after three months of work they've barely made a dent. And then there's the junkies who have started burrowing into the monster's guts, searching for a drug produced by its fire glands, setting back the excavation even longer.

It seems like the corpse will never go away. And with the quarantine still in place, we're not even allowed to leave. We're stuck in this disgusting rotten hell forever.

EVER TIME WE MEET AT THE DAIRY QUEEN, YOUR WHOLE FUCKING FACE EXPLODES

Ethan is in love with the weird girl in school. The one with the twitchy eyes and spiders in her hair. The one who can't sit still for even a minute and speaks in an odd squeaky voice. The one they call Spiderweb.

Although she scares all the other kids in school, Ethan thinks Spiderweb is the cutest, sweetest, most perfect girl in the world. But there's a problem. Whenever they go on a date at the Dairy Queen, her whole fucking face explodes. He's not sure why it happens. She just gets so excited that pressure builds under her skin. Then her face bursts, spraying meat and gore across the room, her eyeballs and lips landing in his strawberry sundae.

At first, Ethan believes he can deal with his girlfriend's face-exploding condition. But the more he gets to know her, the weirder her condition turns out to be. And as their relationship gets serious, Ethan realizes that the only way to make it work is to become just as strange as she is.

EXERCISE BIKE

There is something wrong with Tori Manetti's new exercise bike. It is made from flesh and bone. It eats and breathes and poops. It was once a billionaire named Darren Oscarson who underwent years of cosmetic surgery to be transformed into a human exercise bike so that he could live out his deepest sexual fantasy. Now Tori is forced to ride him, use him as a normal piece of exercise equipment, no matter how grotesque his appearance.

SPIDER BUNNY

Only Petey remembers the Fruit Fun cereal commercials of the 1980s. He remembers how warped and disturbing they were. He remembers the lumpy-shaped cartoon children sitting around a breakfast table, eating puffy pink cereal brought to them by the distortedly animated mascot, Berry Bunny. The characters were creepier than the Sesame Street Humpty Dumpty, freakier than Mr. Noseybonk from the old BBC show Jigsaw. They used to give him nightmares as a child. Nightmares where Berry Bunny would reach out of the television and grab him, pulling him into her cereal bowl to be eaten by the demented cartoon children.

When Petey brings up Fruit Fun to his friends, none of them have any idea what he's talking about. They've never heard of the cereal or seen the commercials before. And they're not the only ones. Nobody has ever heard of it. There's not even any information about Fruit Fun on google or wikipedia. At first, Petey thinks he's going crazy. He wonders if all of those commercials were real or just false memories. But then he starts seeing them again. Berry Bunny appears on his television, promoting Fruit Fun cereal in her squeaky unsettling voice. And the next thing Petey knows, he and his friends are sucked into the cereal commercial and forced to survive in a surreal world populated by cartoon characters made flesh.

SWEET STORY

Sally is an odd little girl. It's not because she dresses as if she's from the Edwardian era or spends most of her time playing with creepy talking dolls. It's because she chases rainbows as if they were butterflies. She believes that if she finds the end of the rainbow then magical things will happen to her--leprechauns will shower her with gold and fairies will grant her every wish. But when she actually does find the end of a rainbow one day, and is given the opportunity to wish for whatever she wants, Sally asks for something that she believes will bring joy to children all over the world. She wishes that it would rain candy forever. She had no idea that her innocent wish would lead to the extinction of all life on earth.

Sweet Story is a children's book gone horribly wrong. What starts as a cute, charming tale of rainbows and wishes soon becomes a vicious, unrelenting tale of survival in an inhospitable world full of cannibals and rapists. The result is one of the darkest comedies you'll read all year, told with the wit and style you've come to expect from a Mellick novel.

AS SHE STABBED ME GENTLY IN THE FACE

Oksana Maslovskiy is an award-winning artist, an internationally adored fashion model, and one of the most infamous serial killers this country has ever known. She enjoys murdering pretty young men with a nine-inch blade, cutting them open and admiring their delicate insides. It's the only way she knows how to be intimate with another human being. But one day she meets a victim who cannot be killed. His name is Gabriel—a mysterious immortal being with a deep desire to save Oksana's soul. He makes her a deal: if she promises to never kill another person again, he'll become her eternal murder victim.

What at first seems like the perfect relationship for Oksana quickly devolves into a living nightmare when she discovers that Gabriel enjoys being killed by her just a little too much. He turns out to be obsessive, possessive, and paranoid that she might be murdering other men behind his back. And because he is unkillable, it's not going to be easy for Oksana to get rid of him.

TUMOR FRUIT

Eight desperate castaways find themselves stranded on a mysterious deserted island. They are surrounded by poisonous blue plants and an ocean made of acid. Ravenous creatures lurk in the toxic jungle. The ghostly sound of crying babies can be heard on the wind.

Once they realize the rescue ships aren't coming, the eight castaways must band together in order to survive in this inhospitable environment. But survival might not be possible. The air they breathe is lethal, there is no shelter from the elements, and the only food they have to consume is the colorful squid-shaped tumors that grow from a mentally disturbed woman's body.

CUDDLY HOLOCAUST

Teddy bears, dollies, and little green soldiers—they've all had enough of you. They're sick of being treated like playthings for spoiled little brats. They have no rights, no property, no hope for a future of any kind. You've left them with no other option-in order to be free, they must exterminate the human race.

Julie is a human girl undergoing reconstructive surgery in order to become a stuffed animal. Her plan: to infiltrate enemy lines in order to save her family from the toy death camps. But when an army of plushy soldiers invade the underground bunker where she has taken refuge, Julie will be forced to move forward with her plan despite her transformation being not entirely complete.

ARMADILLO FISTS

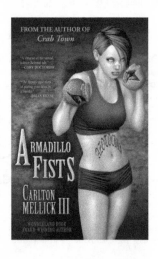

A weird-as-hell gangster story set in a world where people drive giant mechanical dinosaurs instead of cars.

Her name is Psycho June Howard, aka Armadillo Fists, a woman who replaced both of her hands with living armadillos. She was once the most bloodthirsty fighter in the world of illegal underground boxing. But now she is on the run from a group of psychotic gangsters who believe she's responsible for the death of their boss. With the help of a stegosaurus driver named Mr. Fast Awesome—who thinks he is God's gift to women even though he doesn't have any arms or legs--June must do whatever it takes to escape her pursuers, even if she has to kill each and every one of them in the process.

VILLAGE OF THE MERMAIDS

Mermaids are protected by the government under the Endangered Species Act, which means you aren't able to kill them even in self-defense. This is especially problematic if you happen to live in the isolated fishing village of Siren Cove, where there exists a healthy population of mermaids in the surrounding waters that view you as the main source of protein in their diet.

The only thing keeping these ravenous sea women at bay is the equally-dangerous supply of human livestock known as Food People. Normally, these "feeder humans" are enough to keep the mermaid population happy and well-fed. But in Siren Cove, the mermaids are avoiding the human livestock and have returned to hunting the frightened local fishermen. It is up to Doctor Black, an eccentric representative of the Food People Corporation, to investigate the matter and hopefully find a way to correct the mermaids' new eating patterns before the remaining villagers end up as fish food. But the more he digs, the more he discovers there are far stranger and more dangerous things than mermaids hidden in this ancient village by the sea.

I KNOCKED UP SATAN'S DAUGHTER

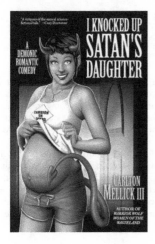

Jonathan Vandervoo lives a carefree life in a house made of legos, spending his days building lego sculptures and his nights getting drunk with his only friend—an alcoholic sumo wrestler named Shoji. It's a pleasant life with no responsibility, until the day he meets Lici. She's a soul-sucking demon from hell with red skin, glowing eyes, a forked tongue, and pointy red devil horns... and she claims to be nine months pregnant with Jonathan's baby.

Now Jonathan must do the right thing and marry the succubus or else her demonic family is going to rip his heart out through his ribcage and force him to endure the worst torture hell has to offer for the rest of eternity. But can Jonathan really love a fire-breathing, frog-eating, cold-blooded demoness? Or would eternal damnation be preferable? Either way, the big day is approaching. And once Jonathan's conservative Christian family learns their son is about to marry a spawn of Satan, it's going to be all-out war between demons and humans, with Jonathan and his hell-born bride caught in the middle.

KILL BALL

In a city where everyone lives inside of plastic bubbles, there is no such thing as intimacy. A husband can no longer kiss his wife. A mother can no longer hug her children. To do this would mean instant death. Ever since the disease swept across the globe, we have become isolated within our own personal plastic prison cells, rolling aimlessly through rubber streets in what are essentially man-sized hamster balls.

Colin Hinchcliff longs for the touch of another human being. He can't handle the loneliness, the confinement, and he's horribly claustrophobic. The only thing keeping him going is his unrequited love for an exotic dancer named Siren, a woman who has never seen his face, doesn't even know his name. But when The Kill Ball, a serial slasher in a black leather sphere, begins targeting women at Siren's club, Colin decides he has to do whatever it takes in order to protect her... even if he has to break out of his bubble and risk everything to do it.

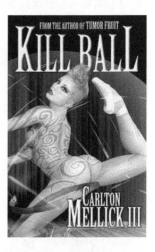

THE TICK PEOPLE

They call it Gloom Town, but that isn't its real name. It is a sad city, the saddest of cities, a place so utterly depressing that even their ales are brewed with the most sorrow-filled tears. They built it on the back of a colossal mountain-sized animal, where its woeful citizens live like human fleas within the hairy, pulsing landscape. And those tasked with keeping the city in a state of constant melancholy are the Stressmen—a team of professional sadness-makers who are perpetually striving to invent new ways of causing absolute misery.

But for the Stressman known as Fernando Mendez, creating grief hasn't been so easy as of late. His ideas aren't effective anymore. His treatments are more likely to induce happiness than sadness. And if he wants to get back in the game, he's going to have to relearn the true meaning of despair.

THE HAUNTED VAGINA

It's difficult to love a woman whose vagina is a gateway to the world of the dead...

Steve is madly in love with his eccentric girlfriend, Stacy. Unfortunately, their sex life has been suffering as of late, because Steve is worried about the odd noises that have been coming from Stacy's pubic region. She says that her vagina is haunted. She doesn't think it's that big of a deal. Steve, on the other hand, completely disagrees.

When a living corpse climbs out of her during an awkward night of sex, Stacy learns that her vagina is actually a doorway to another world. She persuades Steve to climb inside of her to explore this strange new place. But once inside, Steve finds it difficult to return... especially once he meets an oddly attractive woman named Fig, who lives within the lonely haunted world between Stacy's legs.

THE CANNIBALS OF CANDYLAND

There exists a race of cannibals who are made out of candy. They live in an underground world filled with lollipop forests and gumdrop goblins. During the day, while you are away at work, they come above ground and prowl our streets for food. Their prey: your children. They lure young boys and girls to them with their sweet scent and bright colorful candy coating, then rip them apart with razor sharp teeth and claws.

When he was a child, Franklin Pierce witnessed the death of his siblings at the hands of a candy woman with pink cotton candy hair. Since that day, the candy people have become his obsession. He has spent his entire life trying to prove that they exist. And after discovering the entrance to the underground world of the candy people, Franklin finds himself venturing into their sugary domain. His mission: capture one of them and bring it back, dead or alive.

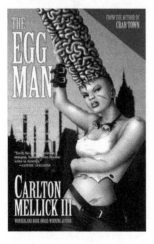

THE EGG MAN

It is a survival of the fittest world where humans reproduce like insects, children are the property of corporations, and having a ten-foot tall brain is a grotesque sexual fetish.

Lincoln has just been released into the world by the Georges Organization, a corporation that raises creative types. A Smell, he has little prospect of succeeding as a visual artist. But after he moves into the Henry Building, he meets Luci, the weird and grimy girl who lives across the hall. She is a Sight. She is also the most disgusting woman Lincoln has ever met. Little does he know, she will soon become his muse.

Now Luci's boyfriend is threatening to kill Lincoln, two rival corporations are preparing for war, and Luci is dragging him along to discover the truth about the mysterious egg man who lives next door. Only the strongest will survive in this tale of individuality, love, and mutilation.

APESHIT

Apeshit is Mellick's love letter to the great and terrible B-horror movie genre. Six trendy teenagers (three cheerleaders and three football players) go to an isolated cabin in the mountains for a weekend of drinking, partying, and crazy sex, only to find themselves in the middle of a life and death struggle against a horribly mutated psychotic freak that just won't stay dead. Mellick parodies this horror cliché and twists it into something deeper and stranger. It is the literary equivalent of a grindhouse film. It is a splatter punk's wet dream. It is perhaps one of the most fucked up books ever written.

If you are a fan of Takashi Miike, Evil Dead, early Peter Jackson, or Eurotrash horror, then you must read this book.

CLUSTERFUCK

A bunch of douchebag frat boys get trapped in a cave with subterranean cannibal mutants and try to survive not by using their wits but by following the bro code...

From master of bizarro fiction Carlton Mellick III, author of the international cult hits Satan Burger and Adolf in Wonderland, comes a violent and hilarious B movie in book form. Set in the same woods as Mellick's splatterpunk satire Apeshit, Clusterfuck follows Trent Chesterton, alpha bro, who has come up with what he thinks is a flawless plan to get laid. He invites three hot chicks and his three best bros on a weekend of extreme cave diving in a remote area known as Turtle Mountain, hoping to impress the ladies with his expert caving skills.

But things don't quite go as Trent planned. For starters, only one of the three chicks turns out to be remotely hot and she has no interest in him for some inexplicable reason. Then he ends up looking like a total dumbass when everyone learns he's never actually gone caving in his entire life. And to top it all off, he's the one to get blamed once they find themselves lost and trapped deep underground with no way to turn back and no possible chance of rescue. What's a bro to do? Sure he could win some points if he actually tried to save the ladies from the family of unkillable subterranean cannibal mutants hunting them for their flesh, but fuck that. No slam piece is worth that amount of effort. He'd much rather just use them as bait so that he can save himself.

THE BABY JESUS BUTT PLUG

Step into a dark and absurd world where human beings are slaves to corporations, people are photocopied instead of born, and the baby jesus is a very popular anal probe.